An Immaculate Conception

An Immaculate Conception

'...Just when you thought it was safe to get on with your own life.'

Trish Clark

IMPERIUM
High Adventure Publishing.com
AUSTRALIA

First published in 2010 by
High Adventure Publishing/ Imperium Books
Tumbulgum, 2490 Australia
© Trish Clark 2010
ISBN10:   0-9807848-5-9
ISBN13:   978-0-9807848-5-5

All rights reserved. No part of this publication may be reproduced, stored in a retrieval system, or transmitted in any form or by any means, electronic, mechanical, photocopying, recording or otherwise, without the prior permission of the publisher.

Cover photograph by Iain Finlay:
A moment of birth,
Roosevelt Hospital, New York City, November 2, 1966

for Dr. Anne Clark

By the same author
   *ANDREA
   *AUSTRALIAN ADVENTURERS
   *MOTHERHOOD
   *CHILDREN OF BLINDNESS

with Iain Finlay
   *AFRICA OVERLAND
   *SOUTH AMERICA OVERLAND
   *ACROSS THE SOUTH PACIFIC
   GOOD MORNING HANOI
   THE SILK TRAIN

Titles marked with an *asterisk were originally published under Trish's previous name, Trish Sheppard.

CONTENTS

CHAPTER	PAGE
ONE	1
TWO	13
THREE	25
FOUR	37
FIVE	53
SIX	69
SEVEN	83
EIGHT	99
NINE	117
TEN	139
ELEVEN	159
TWELVE	181
THIRTEEN	199
FOURTEEN	217
FIFTEEN	231
SIXTEEN	251
SEVENTEEN	273
EIGHTEEN	297
ABOUT THE AUTHOR	315
OTHER TITLES	316

One

Looking back on the day her life changed forever Cathy was always amazed at how it had started out with the same routine she followed every day. There had been no warnings, no hints to give her time for any sort of preparation.

She had drifted into sleep to the sound of the Pacific Ocean eating gently away at the rock face below their bedroom, curled up around Steve. A middle-aged... well, late middle-aged, woman in a successful... well, a non-questioning, marriage with a happily married son and daughter... well her daughter wasn't exactly married but she and her partner had lived together for six years. And she didn't really know if her son and his wife were exactly happy, as she didn't see much of them because they lived such busy lives. But then there was their son, her grandson Sam, joy of her life. No qualifiers there.

Both she and Steve had successful careers, she as a high achiever in the State Education Department and he as a busy self-employed architect. They owned their own home, from where Steve also ran his office. They subscribed to Opera Australia, were Friends of the ABC, bush-walked at weekends and took their annual holidays in Europe. They even made regular calls on her elderly widowed mother, Elizabeth, who lived in Canberra, combining it with visits to the exhibitions at the National Gallery. They were, to those who thought they knew them, a perfect couple. Until on that Friday morning when, as Cathy's brother Tom was quick to point out, with more than a touch of sibling rivalry, it all went to hell in a hand-basket.

She woke at ten to six, as she invariably did, without an alarm clock, some finely tuned internal mechanism, honed by years of habit, bringing her to consciousness. Sliding carefully out of bed so as not to disturb Steve, who did not share her committed passion for the morning light, she left him lying on his back gently snoring. He liked to greet the day more slowly and she knew that by the time she came back he would be shaved, showered and have the coffee and toast ready. They had learned to make adjustments to each other's preferences and three decades plus of practice had honed these skills. The small

CHAPTER ONE

smile she gave as she padded naked down the stairs was a trifle self-satisfied.

'G'day Digger!' she quietly greeted their ebullient blue heeler, who slept in the rumpus room and who was always as eager as she was to get out into the early morning light. He jostled and harrumphed as she slipped on underwear, a tee shirt, shorts and running shoes, whining in excited anticipation, his strong tail thumping against the door. 'Ssshh,' she let him out, following quickly and they both went through the dead-locked gate onto the cliff track, which ran for some kilometres in either direction.

He galloped ahead of Cathy as she loped along gradually increasing her stride as her muscles stretched and warmed. A couple of times he returned to make sure she was following, circled her and took off again, scenting the air, cocking his leg and following tracks accessible only to canine senses, all the while wagging his tail in ferocious pleasure.

By the time they reached the hideously ugly house, which sat squatly on the cliff edge and prevented the track from continuing on, the eastern sky was lightening. She stood on the very edge of the cliff, looking down on the waves crashing over the rocks, breathing hard from exertion and watching as a tanker far out on the horizon ploughed its way south no doubt to Botany Bay to discharge its cargo.

'Look Sam,' she recalled pointing out to her grandson the previous weekend as she was stopped at traffic lights on the beachside drive, 'see the boat, out there at sea.' He was perched beside her on the front seat of the car taking in far more of the bizarre Bondi scene than she thought was good for a four-year old and he turned to fix her with a withering look of contempt. 'Nana! That is not a boat, that is a ship. Boats are small. Ships are big.' The lights had changed and with typical Bondi brashness the teenage male driver behind immediately began to stand on his horn. She edged forwards through the unheeding mass of people and Sam resumed his inspection of the scant clothing and the tattoos on the cosmopolitan crowd all of whom seemed to be cramming food into their mouths while continuing to talk and walk. Without taking his eyes off this non-stop parade Sam added, 'that is the Pacific Ocean and we live on Planet Earth.' He gave her a quick glance to make sure she had taken all that information on board.

She had smiled indulgently then and now she laughed happily out loud at the memory. Digger looked up at her and joined in with a little yelp of joy.

On their return along the cliff top they saw several regulars and exchanged small greetings in passing. There was the Dutchman with the two elegant borzoi hounds. She knew he came from Holland even

CHAPTER ONE

though they had never exchanged more than a dozen words - about their dogs naturally - and those only on rare occasions. He had probably lived in Australia for thirty years but his English still carried the burden of a language that defied all non-nationals to speak it. Then came the young Indian, running as always with his wife. He was a Sikh, Cathy knew, because she had glimpsed his steel bangle. His wife, with her strikingly pale skin and wild red hair was more than likely Irish. They always just raised a hand each in silent greeting. Next was the older Chinese woman in a padded high-collared jacket and pants. Tiny and silent she gave no signals as she walked. Then, just before the pool came the two muscular South African businessmen both in their early thirties, mobile phones on their hips. They ran by at speed but still managed to conduct their first business meeting of the day as they went. Even in her shorts and tee shirt, she knew it was apparent to them that she was not a prospective customer, so they hardly registered her presence. Finally she nodded to a diminutive married couple who looked to be in their early seventies and whose strong features marked them as Eastern Europeans. Appearing weighed down with all that history they trudged rather than walked the track and the husband simply raised his extensive eyebrows in acknowledgement of her.

At the height of summer there would be scores of people walking, running, exercising their dogs, kick boxing, doing press-ups or yoga along this same stretch of coast by this time in the morning. But now, with the winter solstice only two weeks away the numbers had fallen til only the determined and deeply addicted clung to their routine.

'Stay, Digger'. Cathy attached the dog by a leash to a sagging paling. Despite knowing the daily drill he drooped his head in feigned distress. 'You're a rotten con-artist' Cathy chuckled as she fondled his ears. 'I won't be long.'

With the key that allowed members to swim during hours when there was no attendant, she opened the door in the fence surrounding the ocean pool and entered another world. The fence formed a large amphitheatre which caught and held the sound of the ocean so that as she walked down the path the smells, the sounds, the vision, all made her feel as though she was being sucked inexorably into a world of water. Everyday there was a different combination of light, tide and ocean but every day there was the same watery welcome; the same frisson of pure pleasure.

'G'day Mina', she whispered to the three-sided, hollow life-size bronze statue of Wilhelmina Wylie standing on guard at the turn in the path. The daugh-

CHAPTER ONE

ter of the man who'd had the vision to establish the baths in the first decade of the last century Wilhelmina was one of the first female swimmers to represent Australia at an Olympic Games when she and Fanny Durack competed in the 1912 Stockholm Games. Cathy had avoided becoming involved in the venomous bitching and backstabbing amongst the members of the pool committee about the Federation Project, which funded the statue. But once it was in place and the official opening over, the protests had died away. Occasionally some wag gave Mina a swimming cap and goggles or even a bikini top but today she was unadorned.

Along at the far end of the timber deck that hung above the pool was a row of cupboards where regular swimmers stored their personal bits and pieces, kickboards, towels, sunscreen. One fellow, a retired wharfie, even kept an electric jug, instant coffee, tinned milk and a packet of biscuits in his cupboard so as to have a post early-morning-swim caffeine top up. During the day a small cafe operated, serving hot and cold drinks, simple sandwiches, cookies and ice creams.

Cathy had occasionally swum at the baths with Steve during the day. Then there were singles and childless couples who lay about on the deck and around the pool in between cooling dips but it was mostly hordes of ebullient small children splashing and yelling watched over by parents who chose the pool over the beach for its comparative safety. On those visits in full daylight hours it was a totally different place that she in no way associated with the splendour of her early morning ritual.

With a sense of growing urgency she quickly removed her swimming gear from her cupboard and stuffed her speedily stripped running clothes back in. There was no one else in the pool: just how she loved it; allowing her to wallow in a feeling of full possession. In mounting excitement and pleasure she ran lightly down the wooden steps to the rocky surrounds, made her way quickly to the far wall, hurriedly pulled on her cap and goggles and as the first sliver of orange sun appeared over the horizon dove into the welcoming embrace of the water.

The first fifty-metre lap was always a combination of shock and settling in. The water temperature had dropped since high summer but it still hovered around 17 degrees. It wouldn't fall to a chilly 15 for another couple of months. By the return lap she was steadied in the water and stroking strongly, breathing both sides as she had been coached to do when she swam for her school. Today all the elements came together in perfection. There were no ocean storms to pick up the waves. Across the top of the wall as she

CHAPTER ONE

turned her head she caught snap-shot glimpses of Wedding Cake Island seemingly floating on a calm surface a few hundred metres offshore. It was mid-tide so the ocean lapped imperceptibly over the wall into the pool, sparkling in the steadily rising sunlight as it did so. And as she brought her arm out to stroke forward the drips falling from her skin glistened golden. Cathy was aware of being deeply happy.

The uneven floor of the pool unreeled beneath her; jumbled rocks, opened oyster shells, sea urchins, and small squads of colourless fish drifting with the pull of the water. Up and down the pool she went, stretching her arms out as far as possible, pulling her body along in a sinuous glide, making neat, strong kicks with her feet, 'keep yer bloody kick down, keep yer bloody kick down', she recalled her coach yelling at her and smiled into the water, automatically ticking off the number of turns, until, oops! What was that! A dark streamlined shape cut quickly through the water to cross in front of her. Oh bloody hell! She froze mid-stroke. Instinctively she tried to hold her arms up as she trod water. Her stomach knotted in fear and she could feel her pulse beating wildly behind her ear. Was that her scream she heard? Then pop! Up beside her bobbed a shag. Just as suddenly it turned its long, sinuous black neck down under the water again. She thrust her face in and watched as it chased a little shoal of fish, its sleek streamlined shape powering effortlessly through the water. Phew! She let out her held breath and gave a little laugh as she slowly resumed her stroking.

By the time she had completed a kilometre, she had been joined by a couple of other diehards. They exchanged congratulatory raised arm salutes in passing. The thin band of light cloud on the horizon had turned from the softest pink to an almost harsh gold as the earth continued its revolution into the sun's embrace. The sky became steadily lighter and what lay beneath the water became increasingly revealed. Cathy continued her mind-empty communion with the elements until she had covered a further kilometre, then stripped off her cap, shook out her hair and submerged one last time so as to feel the water on her scalp. As she pulled herself up the metal steps onto the surround, feeling the weighty gravity of the other world return she glanced up to see Daisy on the upper deck performing her own regular early morning ritual by spreading out bowls for the wild cat which roamed the area and stopped by at this time for its daily feed.

'G'day Daisy,' she greeted the older woman as she stood and towelled herself down. Daisy nodded and took no notice as Cathy quickly stripped off her bathers and slipped back into her shorts and top. The two women had been greeting each other in the

CHAPTER ONE

early mornings like this for several years. Over this time they had built up a bare-bones picture of each other's lives. Cathy knew Daisy had been a widow for some years, lived alone in a flat she owned in the red brick apartment block opposite the pool, that she had one daughter who lived on her own in the Blue Mountains and that she had two grandchildren.

Daisy knew what work Cathy and her husband did. She knew their children's names and something of their lives and she had met Sam by chance when they were all getting takeaways at 'Chish and Fips', the kiosk on the promenade, one summer evening.

She'd made a great fuss of him, insisting against Cathy's wishes on giving him a two-dollar coin, 'to buy some lollies with'. Cathy had not held her ground partly because she hated to make a scene in public, but also because she knew Daisy's gesture came about because she so badly wanted to have a great-grandchild. This seemed unlikely because, as she had told Cathy, her grandson showed no signs of ever getting married and her granddaughter, Ruby, was in a lesbian relationship.

Their conversations had skirted politely around this situation. Testing each other. Trying on ideas for size. Cathy being gently solicitous in an attempt to console Daisy for what the other woman obviously felt as a tremendous sense of loss. 'It's the end of the line,' she had cried one morning. 'A one-way street. Its all over for me.'

This morning Cathy could see that Daisy was happy, in fact was bursting with happiness and waiting to share the source of this joy with her. Infected by the other woman's pleasure and in total innocence of an answer that would shake the foundations of her life, Cathy beamed at her and asked, 'Well come on then Daisy, out with it. Why so happy?'

The elderly woman was so excited she did a little tap routine before flinging her still sinewy arms around Cathy. 'Oh thank you, thank you!' she cried. Amazed, if not a little stunned, Cathy managed to mumble into the suffocating embrace.
'Thank you? Thank you for what? Daisy moved away to hold her at arms' length.

'For what?' Tears of joy filled the eyes of the older woman. 'For what?' she repeated. 'For your Lewis agreeing to father my great-grandson. That's what.'

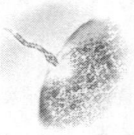

Two

'What's happened?! What's the matter? Tell me! Tell me! Are you alright?! Are you hurt? Where?'

Cathy had flung herself up the stairs and collapsed onto Steve where he stood in their kitchen, sending the coffee pot spiralling along the granite top into the sink. Clinging to him she had begun to sob, able at last to let go of the emotions, which she had kept pent up on the run back from the pool.

Daisy's obvious joy had made it impossible for her to appear other than equally delighted. The fact that Daisy assumed Cathy knew of Lewis's 'great act of Christian love and charity,' made it all the more impossible for her to express her true feelings.

But what were her true feelings? From the jumbled, mish-mashed quagmire of questions and emotions which hurricaned around inside her brain while she stood smiling at Daisy only one word came through constant and loud and that was a resounding NO.

Daisy was talking animatedly and Cathy had tried to focus. Medical procedures, clinics, lesbian self-help groups, do-it-yourself methods were all mentioned. Church objections, the greying of Australia, the Blue Mountains, female Governor General, female Prime-Minister and female State Premiers and somehow even the price of Sydney real estate bubbled forth. But then, Cathy found herself thinking distractedly, how could there ever be a conversation about anything in Sydney that somehow or other did not include at least a passing reference to Sydney real estate prices.

'I have to go Daisy or I'll be late for work.' She could hear Digger whining and straining on his leash.

Daisy, fairly exploding with happiness, engulfed Cathy in another hug. 'Grandmothers and great-grandmothers of the world unite,' she called after Cathy as she fled up the path.

Cathy was hardly more coherent than Daisy had been as she tried to give Steve the news.

'Well that's a relief,' he gave her a squeeze before letting go, 'from the way you were carrying on I

CHAPTER TWO

thought you'd been raped, or at the very least stung by blue-bottles.'

She stared at him in disbelief as he began mopping up the coffee. 'Carrying on? Is that all you can say?'

Well, what...? I mean, how...? what the hell does Claudia have to say about it?' How can Lewis be fathering a child with...? Hey hang on a minute, isn't Daisy's grand-daughter a lesbian or something?'

Cathy wiped her eyes and smoothed down her tee shirt.

'I have never met the girl and I didn't even know that Lewis had.' Her voice had a cool edge. 'And yes she is a lesbian. So your grandchild will be raised by two lesbians. What do you think about that?'

Steve looked up from wiping smears of coffee off the cupboard fronts and faced his wife in the hardening morning light. Into the intense resounding silence, which stood between them, came the ringing of the phone. Neither of them made a move to answer it even though it sat just to one side of the pantry, beside the toaster. Three rings, the whirring of the tape readying itself to take a message and then a disembodied voice boomed forth.

'G'day Cathy! This is Tom. Remember me. I'm your brother. Yeh, yeh I know its all my fault. I don't return your calls. Sorry about that. But I really need to talk to you. Today. Like it's important. Thought I'd get you before you left for work. Can't find your work or mobile number. I can't find any bloody thing actually. Hopeless. Always been hopeless. Can't seem to get it together. Not like you. But I do need to talk to you so if you're still there pick up the phone...and if you're gone already I'll call Steve later when I can find his work number and get your work number fr...' the message tape cut him dead.

'You'd better have your shower,' Steve moved back to the coffee pot, 'I'll make a fresh cup and you can take some toast and a banana with you in the car. I'll call Tom later and give him your mobile number. Needs his big sister. Sounded a bit wound up.' He moved towards her, 'Perhaps we are too,' but she had already turned and moved away, as he added, 'so lets talk about all this tonight when you've calmed down.'

'When you've calmed down,' she repeated the words out loud to herself as she eased across into one of the faster traffic lanes in which vehicles were edging their way across the Bridge. She didn't feel like calming down. She felt like screaming. Not at anyone in particular. Just screaming. She opened her mouth and tried. But nothing came out. Inhibited, she sneered at herself and tried again. Still nothing. 'You're pathetic,' she reprimanded herself aloud.

CHAPTER TWO

Perhaps Lewis had made this same assessment and that was the reason why he hadn't told her himself; why he had left her to find out from Daisy. Or was it simply because she counted for so little in his life; this man whom she had raised from baby through boy to man? At what point did a child feel that it wasn't necessary to even have a discussion before making such a huge, vast, far-ranging decision. Yes, it would be his baby, or at least he would be the father, or anyway the biological father. But she, Cathy, would be the grandmother. Did what she felt about that count for nothing?

She turned the car down into the car park under her office and realised that she couldn't even recall the last twenty minutes of the drive.

'Good morning Ms. Stuart,' the commissionaire greeted her as she came out into the lobby. He raised his finger to slow her stride. 'You have a visitor waiting in your office.' Cathy frowned. This was highly irregular. The man smiled his apologies. 'She was most insistent that it would be alright with you, it's your daughter.'

'I feel like shit,' was Sophie's reply to her mother's inquiry, 'and I know that's how I look. ' She grimaced. She'd obviously been crying. Her face was bloated and pale, her hair unwashed and limp. She was huddled into what Cathy recalled had once been the elegant, full-length, camel hair overcoat she'd bought on her first solo trip to Europe when she was fresh out of college. She and Steve had waved her away at the airport, a beautiful twenty-two year old taking off to conquer the world. Bubbling with schemes, dreams and enthusiasms. So keen to get on with life she hadn't even turned for a last glimpse of them as she went through to the immigration counters. With a shock Cathy now looked at her daughter, slumped in the visitors' chair and for the first time saw her as a nearly middle-aged woman. The camel coat looked like a bag lady's dressing gown.

Cathy took off her honey-coloured woollen jacket, hung it over the back of her seat. She rearranged at her neck the piece of dot-painted silk an Aboriginal teaching colleague had given to her and which so perfectly set off the understated simple line of her matching dress. Her eyes did a quick skim of her desktop. She could feel herself slip on her other personality. Here she was no longer Mrs. Cathy Connolly. She became Ms. Catherine Stuart. This was her empire. Without needing to check her diary she knew her first meeting was in twenty minutes.

From the top drawer of her desk she handed her daughter a box of facial refresher tissues and a small hairbrush. They were a part of what she called

CHAPTER TWO

her small emergency kit, which she kept handy less for herself than for the parents, students and teachers who flowed through her room like a river of sorrow.

Sophie warded off the proffered comfort and shrank further back into her crumpled overcoat.

'It'll make you feel better darling.'

'It will not.' Sophie blew her nose loudly into an already soggy tissue.

Cathy left the box and brush on the desk top and asked, 'So, what's happened?'

'Jeff's gone.'

'Gone where?'

"I don't know. And I don't give a flying fuck.' Tears poured down her cheeks. 'He's left me. This time it's for good. We had a big argument. I told him he had to make up his mind. Really make up his mind. Forever stuff. Marriage. Children. Or goodbye. Mum! I'm thirty-three. We've been together since I was twenty-five. Most of my adult life. It's time. He keeps saying to give him more time. But I have. You know last year he took off with his mates and went skiing in bloody Val d'Isere or wherever. To get it out of his system, whatever IT is. All they did was get drunk and screw French tarts. What a deadshit. Oh fuck everything!

Cathy remembered Sophie's English teacher telling her that her daughter had a very good command of the language.

'I really have given him a chance. Tried not to be too pushy, too demanding. When he lost his job last year...it wasn't his fault the company went belly-up...I didn't nag him to look for another one straightaway. He said he needed a bit of a holiday. That it would take time for the market to pick up again. That he wanted to visit his mum. So he went up to her place at Hastings Point and did some surfing and hung out. This time it was Aussie tarts. He only admitted it to me because one of his drunken mates had already told me. Even then I thought we could work it out. Fed him. Fucked him. Tried to give him his space. Paid the rent. Paid the bills. All that crap. And you know what? It is crap. But he's just....'

'Immature,' Cathy suggested.

'Yes. But I love him.' Sophie resumed weeping. 'I love him'

'Sophie, you love what you want him to be, not what he is.'

'Mum! For god's sake!' It was a scream. Sophie pushed back and rose so quickly that her trailing coat became entangled in the leg of the chair, which toppled over and crashed into the wall almost taking Sophie with it. She dragged herself free.

CHAPTER TWO

Cathy found that she was glad her room had been chosen as the most sound-proof and the one furthest from the open-plan main office, on the grounds that her clients would both appreciate this degree of privacy and as well cause as little disruption as possible to other staff.

'I'm your daughter. I'm not one of your bloody clients or whatever you bloody well call them these days. Don't try your psycho-babble jargon, bullshit chatter on me. Good God next you'll be telling me there are plenty more pebbles on the beach, or some other totally unhelpful cliché. You think I don't know all this stuff? You think I'm stupid?'

She paced to and fro, then stopped as she pulled a cigarette packet from her coat pocket shook out a cigarette lit it with the lighter that followed, inhaled deeply and with obvious relish blew clouds of sweet smelling bluish smoke out through her nose.

'I know. Its a fucking non-smoking area.' she grimaced.

'I didn't know you had gone back to smoking.'

'Well. There you go. I guess there's a lot of things you don't know about your daughter.' The cigarette seemed to have calmed her. In a quieter voice she said, 'I'm glad Jeff has gone really. In my head I've known for ages that it was never going to come to anything. He's just a kid. We had some good times. But he was never going to settle down. You just don't know how hard it is to find the right man nowadays. They're all either married, losers, or gay. Look who's talking clichés now. But it's true. Maybe I've left my run too late.'

She stubbed the cigarette out and began to cry softly. The two women embraced. 'I'm not like you Mum. I just don't seem to be able to get it together.'

Cathy closed her eyes, hearing her brother's phone message. 'Can't seem to get it together.'

'I want a baby Mum. A family, actually. Wouldn't you like another grandchild?'

'Uh-huh,' Cathy nodded her head. 'And it seems I'm having one.'

Sophie's eye's widened. 'That's great! I haven't seen Claudia for ages. When's she due?'

'Claudia won't be the mother,' Cathy said quietly and before her daughter could register surprise, 'Lewis is going to be the father but the mother is a lesbian. She's Daisy Jacob's grand-daughter.'

'Ruby?!'

'You know her?'

'Yes, yes. I've known her for a couple of years. Her gran had a hip op. And she used to bring her to the rehab pool for physio. We got along well right off the bat so I invited her over to our place. Jeff didn't take to her. Made vile comments about skirt-lifters.

CHAPTER TWO

So I started visiting her place by myself when he was out with his drunken mates. We went out with her pals and did lots of low life stuff together. You know that beyond-beyond mainstream theatre and the Newtown cheap eats caffs. It was me who introduced her to Claudia and Lewis. We all went up to the Blue Mountains for a weekend. Her Mum has a bit of land up there.'

She looked considerably more cheerful. 'Well. That's great. Good on you Lewis spreading the Connolly sperm around. Oops sorry, the Stuart/Connolly sperm.' She managed a little laugh.

'Perhaps that's what I should do. Get on with a lesbian and go the IVF route. Pardon the pun.'

Cathy moved back behind her desk and sat down.

Sophie looked at her. 'No. Perhaps not. Can't really imagine coming at the physical stuff with a woman. Can you?'

Cathy shook her head and then said, 'the baby's not even underway yet. But its what they have planned. So, what do you think about your niece or nephew being raised by two lesbians?'

'What's the difference? They'll be great Mums. You'll really like Ruby. She's funny and warm. And Kit, that's her partner, she's terrific too. Very responsible, intelligent. Good job, caring, supportive. If she was a bloke, she'd be perfect. But you can't have everything and don't I know that! Good old Lewis. Who would have thought it? Bit of a dark horse isn't he?'

Cathy nodded and started to move papers on her desk.

'I get the hint Mum. Distraught daughter has to make way for others exhibiting even more inappropriate behaviour. Right?! ' She sounded positively light-hearted. Turning back from the door she placed her cigarettes and lighter on the desk. 'Won't be needing those anymore. Not good for a foetus . I'm off to hunt down a man to father me some babies. That's what Australia needs isn't it?'

Three

The meeting bordered on being a fiasco. For some months Cathy had sensed growing dissatisfaction, a rumbling discontent brewing around her. Overheard remarks, casual innuendos, conversations abruptly terminated when she chanced to appear unexpectedly.

'This place is like a harem, or a bloody nunnery,' her friend Pat Martin had commented recently. 'Not healthy having all these women cooped up together.' The two women, who had known each other a long time having gone through teachers' college together back in the days of their Canberra youth, were having a lunchtime sandwich together in a small café near their office. 'Shouldn't be surprised if we didn't all menstruate in unison!'

Cathy smiled at her friend's remarks. She tried to put aside, as unworthy of herself as a woman, the idea that the Department would run more smoothly if there was less gender discrepancy.

She said, 'It's not funny really and I agree, its not natural.'

Pat continued. 'When I left hands-on teaching to come work in the office I thought that one of the pluses would be that at least there would be a few blokes around but its as bad in there as it is in the classroom.'

Cathy gave a small sigh, 'Yes... and that's why I worry about Sam. He starts school next year and with the teaching environment as it is, its more than likely that he'll spend the next twelve years of his life, the formative years, under the guiding supervision of women. Not good.' She shook her head.

'Lewis and Claudia will send him to private school, at least in high school years.' Pat said, more as a statement than a question. 'There are a lot more male teachers in the private sector.'

Cathy sighed again. 'Yes, I guess that's what they'll do, but not everyone has that choice.'

'One of the things I admire about you,' Pat gave her colleague a friendly pat on the arm as they stood up to return to the office, 'is the way that over the years you haven't let experience dim your belief in public education. The continual cost-cutting, no matter which political party has been in power, the u-

CHAPTER THREE

turns in education policy, the changing fads and fashions; remember that period when learning to spell went out the window, all that mattered was that the little darlings express themselves!'

Both women laughed and Cathy said, 'I think we imported that particular idea from England. But over the years we've brought in equally ludicrous ideas from the States.'

'I bet that, even now,' Pat said with a grin, 'you still believe in free public education of the highest standard being readily available for everyone.'

Cathy nodded. 'I certainly do.'

'I still remember the way you used to talk like that when we were in training.' Pat's grin widened. 'You are a prime example of hope winning out over experience!'

'You mean I'm a fool.'

'An admirable fool,' her friend concluded.

Cathy knew that many people in the Department shared Pat's cynicism. She just hadn't expected the meeting to get so personal.

It was Jane Howard who seemed to be at the nub of the conflict. Immediately she joined the Learning Support Team it was apparent Jane was highly intelligent, hard working and politically savvy. She was also a dry, prickly character and Cathy had many times mentally cursed herself for getting offside with her when they were very first introduced by making what had been intended as a casually humorous remark.

'So you were not beheaded after all.'
Jane had pursed her lips. Cathy had blundered on.
'I guess you've heard all the Jane Howard-Henry VIII jokes there are.'

Jane had nodded in dismissive acquiescence. 'And just to forestall any further ribaldry at my expense I should let you know that my partner's name is Henrietta.'

There had been sounds of barely muffled amusement from other staff members at the table.

Now Cathy glanced around that same table and formally opened the meeting, which she had called in her capacity as Acting Assistant Director of Department.

She had been designated Acting Assistant Director eight months previously. With the increase in work load and responsibilities had come a larger salary and consequent increase in future superannuation pay out. She had been pleased to step up to the mark not just because it showed an appreciation of her skills but also because, very far back in her mind, she had started to sense for the first time the inkling of an idea that she was beginning to approach the home

CHAPTER THREE

stretch in her career. She had put it well aside as an unwelcome concept because she loved her work. It was a big part of how she saw herself. She could not imagine a Catherine Stuart who was not in full-time, worthwhile employment. Even so, a seed idea seemed to have planted itself and to have a life of its own. Along with it had come apprehension.

For the first time in her long career Cathy admitted to herself, and only herself, that she was anxious about whether or not she would be confirmed in her job. This was something that in the past she would not have given a passing thought to, simply assuming that she would be. But this time the interviews and weeding out process had taken an unusually long time and the Director of Department, Claude Borsellino, had mentioned, a little too casually Cathy thought, that competition for the position was fierce and had included applicants from interstate.

With the habit of a tidy mind developed over the years she put all these thoughts aside as the meeting began. The next hour was spent discussing a number of particularly difficult client/Department relationships in the hope that broadening the input of ideas could help solve what seemed to be intransigent cases.

AN IMMACULATE CONCEPTION

'Teaching the teachers,' was how Cathy explained it when asked in social situations about what work she did within the Department. 'I have a group of eight specially trained people; all of them are also highly qualified teachers, who are in essence troubleshooters. They can be called in by any teacher anywhere in the Sydney metropolitan area to give back-up in situations they feel are getting beyond their capacity to control.'

If questioned further she went on to explain that, 'the work requires plenty of diplomatic skills as well as a great deal of experience in actual teaching. The situations we most commonly deal with involve providing support for teachers faced with students who are reported as being in Oppositional Defiance.'

By this stage most purely superficial inquiries ceased.

'They don't really want to know, ' Cathy had commented to Steve one evening on the drive home from dinner at a friend's home. Her husband, who'd heard these complaints innumerable times before, merely murmured understandingly as he slowed down at the approach to their home. 'Most parents treat schools like babysitting centres. They pass over all responsibility for their children to teachers and we only ever hear from them when a problem develops.'

CHAPTER THREE

The most difficult problem case for the group on this occasion was a confronting one, particularly for the slightly built woman teacher concerned. She had been faced with a 182cm., heavy set, foul-mouthed fifteen-year-old boy masturbating during class and handing out photographs of his naked sixteen-year-old sister.

Pat Martin, the most senior member of the group, and therefore quite incidentally, also automatically on the short list of applicants for Cathy's job, was the staff member who had been designated by Cathy to this particular situation.

'Over the past three months, ' Pat explained to the others seated around her, 'I've tried everything possible. I've been out to the school at least once a week, every week. I've sat in on this teacher's class. I've stayed back after school to give her some words of encouragement. I've made some suggestions to her about how to deal with this particular pupil. And I tried to do this with some sensitivity so as to not undermine her sense of self-worth and competency, which I can assure you is running at an all time low.'

The other staff members looked concerned. Some of them made notes. Pat continued.

'I've met with the head teacher and the school counsellor, both of whom are at their wit's end. And,' she paused for emphasis, 'I've met with the parents.

They're Lebanese. The father is a self-employed electrician. His one suggestion was that his son leave school. His actual words were,' Pat consulted her notes, 'He's not a kid any longer. He should get a proper job and pull his weight.' The mother told me,' again Pat looked at her notes, 'my boy is not the one with the problem. It's the fault of all those other boys. What can you expect, they're Greek Orthodox.' Pat shut her notebook.

'The pupil has been put on notice by the Department. Told that if he doesn't modify his behaviour he will be disciplined. We all know that means he will be expelled. But his behaviour has not improved and, right as I speak, the teacher is on the point of quitting.'

There were some expressions of sympathy for Pat and for the teacher. But not from Jane Howard, who said, 'You should encourage her to quit.'

The others looked surprised and the male staff member asked why.

'She's obviously not up to it. Teaching. She should leave now, take the softer option in a career more suited to her sensibilities. It's not going to get any easier. Teaching is a rough business and certain to get rougher. You only have to look at the stats . Over-indulged children, soft, uninvolved, or more probably absent, parents and culturally mixed

CHAPTER THREE

schools. A recipe for this sort of behaviour.' All this said in a harsh tone, which bordered on being provocative.

Cathy tried to calm the atmosphere by asking for suggestions from those around the table as to how they would approach the situation. She sensed an unwillingness to speak.

Into the silence Pat told them 'That teacher is in her late thirties. Divorced with two young children. She's a good teacher, a woman who takes her responsibilities seriously. We need to support her, not encourage her to throw it all away. There's her super. She's built it up for fifteen years. She'd have to retrain for some entirely new career. Start from scratch. Not easy, as many of us know, when you are approaching your middle years. What else has her degree in education made her suitable for?

'She could open a knitting wool shop.' Jane blandly suggested.

Pat expressed her disgust at such flippancy.

"I'm not trying to be being flippant,' Jane shot back. 'I'm stating the obvious. This woman is in the wrong business. You've forgotten what its like out there.'

Spluttering with indignation Pat responded,' Excuse me, Miss Howard,' there was an emphasis on the Miss, 'may I remind you that after I completed my degree I was offered a cadetship, due to the high level of marks I had attained, for further studies on full pay for a degree in special education specialising in educational studies which enabled me to teach the most physically and mentally disabled through to the most gifted. And that, for almost thirty years, until I was seconded to this office, is what I did. I have more experience than most;' she paused to let the implied reference to her adversary make impact, "out there,' as you insist on referring to our school system.'

Jane Howard was completely unflustered by this counter-attack. 'I say again that its changed and its continuing to change, faster than anyone anticipated. Its five years and four months since you were a class teacher. Also all your teaching was done on the North Shore where we have our problems, but I think everyone here would agree they are somewhat softer than in other areas, like the one we have been discussing.'

Pat and Cathy exchanged glances. Both women wondering how Jane Howard had come by this personal information.

'I am the first to admit,' Jane went on, 'that when I was offered this job in the State Office as a Project Officer specialising in Behaviour and Attendance, I jumped at it as light relief from the teaching position I'd held in Western Sydney for fifteen years.

CHAPTER THREE

The same amount of time as the teacher you are trying to help. I understand she may well be at a breaking point. She's done well to last for fifteen years. It's more usually ten and then perhaps another seven and then it speeds up to five and on to three. I've watched it happen. I could write a thesis on it.'

The ripple of movement among the other women at the table seemed to be one of agreement with this assessment.

Jane continued. 'I consider this job a breather. A way of collecting my strength for the assault course. If I don't get promotion within this group,' she looked at Cathy who managed not to flinch, 'I'll go back out there and go for an Assistant Principal post and so hopefully on up the ladder so that I can get the best super package too. I may not have children, but I do have other responsibilities which I also take seriously.'

There was a shuffling of files and papers and to the obvious relief of everyone, bar Jane Howard; Cathy closed the meeting with some general words of encouragement.

Pat hung back so that she and Cathy were left alone in the room together.

'Uppity bitch!' she grimaced. 'You want to watch out. She's after your job. Bit disappointing how successfully she's managed the divide and rule game.

AN IMMACULATE CONCEPTION

Got a few on her side I'd say. But you'll see her off. You want to grab a sandwich outside?'

'I'd love to but I've been booked by my brother for a whingeing session. That's not kind but you know what I mean.'

'I do indeed. Give him my love. No better not. Just my regards. Perhaps I should have married him when he asked me all those years ago. Remember that? God we were so young.' They both smiled. 'I could have lived the life of self-indulgence his wife has. No need to work. Nor cope with the rudeness of Miss...' again the emphasis, '...Jane Howard. And anyway, what's she got against knitting wool shops, that's what I'd like to know.'

Then they both really laughed because the two of them were avid knitters.

Four

The café was jam-packed with the North Sydney lunchtime crowd. The early winter weather was still warm enough to encourage some of the men to remove their suit jackets which revealed a peacock array of subtly coloured business shirts set off by carefully chosen ties. Tone on tone seemed to be the go, with soft lilac on a quiet purple being the trendsetter.

And the women all in black, Cathy thought as she people-watched from a table to one side of the open entrance way.

She had asked Claudia about this monotone approach to female dressing one recent early evening when her daughter-in-law had come by to pick up Sam whom Cathy had been caring for after kindergarten for the couple of extra hours which Claudia had needed to spend at her office. Lewis seemed to be out of town.

AN IMMACULATE CONCEPTION

Claudia had arrived in full black. 'Women who wear colour are not taken seriously,' she had responded. Claudia worked in advertising, which was an area of life Cathy found astounding that anyone could take seriously. 'And its so much easier. It's one less thing to think about. You just put it on and its done.'

She made sure Sam had fastened his seat belt before going around to the driver's seat. As Claudia settled behind the wheel Sam let down his window.

'Love you Nana!' He blew her a kiss. Cathy's heart surged. Claudia gave a peremptory wave and they were gone.

'You look pretty pleased with life,' Tom stood at the chair beside her.

'I was just thinking about Sam.'

'Ah yes. The golden grandson.' The tone was a touch envious. 'What will you eat?'

'Just a pumpkin soup, thanks.'

'Will you share a bruschetta?'

'Okay.'

She watched him weave his way among the scrum at the counter to place their order.

Tom was only just on a year younger than her. She had always assumed she and her brother were home leave babies; conceived both in hurried lust and with an unconscious desire to replace what had been

CHAPTER FOUR

lost. Mother Gaia at work. Not that she had ever even considered asking their mother if this was the case. Those were matters that remained locked up inside her mother's heart after she was widowed at twenty-five, when her army officer husband had been killed in action, while serving with Australian forces in Korea.

Elizabeth had never discussed the tragedy of their father's death during the final night battle of Samichon River fought with extraordinary ferocity, and seeming disregard for human lives on the part of the Chinese commanders, a mere thirty-six hours before the signing of the final armistice which brought an end to the hostilities. Their mother's response had always been that one just got on with life. Didn't make a fuss. To do so was considered vulgar and in bad taste.

The one overt concession made to emotion was that Tom was named after Thomas Samuel, the father who had died before he was born. Sam too bore his grandfather's name.

As he made his way back through the crowd Tom became entangled in a chair or table leg and almost lost his footing. There was some good-natured, though sharpish, chiacking from the tableful of young men and it was then that Cathy noticed her brother didn't look his usual self. His shirt was bloused out under his jacket, his tie a little askew and his colour heightened. As he took his seat, facing her, with his back to the other table, she smelt alcohol.

'Pushy young Turks,' he muttered. 'They're from my office. Circling like sharks. Waiting for me to step aside or move on out. See the one in the broad-striped shirt with the white collar?'

Cathy had noticed. He was particularly handsome. Though, she judged, somewhat ebullient and keen on himself.

'He had the bloody nerve the other day to ask me if I played golf and when I said no he asked, 'Bowls then.' Cathy didn't respond, unwilling to be deflected by such tactics.

Tom licked his lips. Cathy poured him a glass of water fixed him with a keen look and asked,

'So?'

Tom swallowed and pursed his lips awkwardly, then breathed out heavily. Cathy spontaneously turned her head a little to avoid the full blast of whisky breath.

'Sorry sis.' he said in a low voice, sounding as if he meant it. 'But I really needed it.'

'Its alright,' she tried to make light of the confession. ' Just a bit sort of...' she shrugged, 'hard to take at this time of the day.' She smiled at him in what she hoped was an encouraging way. It occurred to her

CHAPTER FOUR

that she had been doing this all her life and that it had not made any long-term difference. It seemed to be a pattern they couldn't break out of. She thought with a touch of wistful anger that she couldn't recall one occasion on which he had asked her how her life was going. There seemed to be a tacit assumption on his part that her life was always going well. While his life staggered from crisis to crisis. And here she was once more, following the same old game plan. The one set up when they were needy children of a distant widowed mother and she had taken up the role of substitute parent.

'So?' she heard herself ask again as the server of the soup and bruschetta came and went. When there was no response she prompted, 'Is it work? Is it Deidre? Is it the girls? Is it your health? You certainly don't look too good.' When there was still no response she fell back on an attempt at humour. 'I know. You've fallen in love with a thirty-year-old.'

'Thirty-three actually.'

She had returned to the office, shut herself away in her room and tried unsuccessfully to examine papers on intra and inter-departmental cost-cutting suggestions which Claude Borsellino had dropped by, remarking in a tired manner, 'All that matters now is the bottom line. On top of everything else we're expected to be accountants too. Most of the time it seems that has to be given priority over all else.'

Cathy had tried to bring some sense to the figures but found she couldn't concentrate. Her mind was awash with the emotions stirred up by the day's family news. So she took an early mark, telling herself that she didn't care if Jane Howard noticed, and surprised Steve by being home early enough for them to sit rugged up on the deck as the light went out of sky.

'THIRTY-THREE,' Steve exploded when she told him about her lunchtime conversation with her brother. ' Bloody hell! What is the man thinking about.' Digger, lying at his feet, lifted his head and looked at Steve as if shocked by his language.

'He's not thinking *about* anything,' Cathy finished her wine. 'He's thinking *with* his dick. That's what he's doing.'

'Bloody hell,' Steve repeated, more quietly. With a shake of his head. Digger settled his head back between his paws. 'Does Deidre know?

'Yes.'

'And?'

'She's given him a month to make up his mind; to choose between them. And she's agreed not to mention it to the girls until then.

'Pretty civilised.'

CHAPTER FOUR

'Pretty clever. She's many things, is Deidre. But she's not a fool.'

There had never been much more than a socially acceptable level of politeness between Cathy and her brother's wife. Cathy thought Deidre was shallow and indulged. Deidre's response was to be underwhelmed by Cathy's professional achievements and to subtly insinuate that being a full-time mother to her and Tom's daughters showed infinitely better value judgement and grasp of a woman's role.

'She doesn't want to settle for having to get by on only half of what they own. She enjoys the role of Mosman matron. Playing tennis, doing lunch, cultivating her garden, giving dinner parties for Tom's business colleagues. Visiting the needy.'

'Catharine!' Steve's tone was sharp with reprimand and Cathy knew she had overstepped the mark.

'Yes. Well,' she responded sheepishly. 'Maybe I was being a bit too harsh. But you know she has lived a life totally sheltered from the realities most people have to face. So perhaps this will come as a bit of a wake up call.'

Steve's silence was a rebuke.

'Well, tell me what she has ever done that's added to the sum total of life.' Cathy asked.

'Oh God, you can be judgemental sometimes. And lets face it, what have any of us done?' Steve raised his hand to slow her response. 'None of us are Nelson Mandela. And what Deidre has done is the best she can, within her capabilities, limited though you may find those to be. And stop screwing your face around like that. I know you well enough to know that means you realise some of what I am saying is right. She has been an excellent mother. From the time they were born she gave those girls her full, undivided attention. She pushed them through school, kept them out of harm's way and made damn sure they did well enough to get into uni. And she didn't stop there. She gave them all the back up and support they needed till they earned their degrees and got a start in life. She made them her full-time career and she made a damn good job of it. She can be proud of what she's achieved.'

'Good heavens.' Cathy was genuinely surprised. 'I had no idea you liked her so much.'

'I don't,' Steve was emphatic. 'I find her company very tedious. She's the female equivalent of a pompous prick. Her social attitudes can at times be repugnant and I admit there have been occasions when I have hoped that something like this would happen to her just to knock her off her sanctimonious perch. But now its occurred, I find I feel sorry for her.'

CHAPTER FOUR

Cathy reached across for her husband's hand. 'You're a good bloke... and I promise to try to be less of a bitch.'

'Don't try too hard,' he smiled, 'there are elements of it I like. And I should own up to feeling relieved that if they really do split up, then we won't have to attend any more of those ghastly parties she gives.'

They both laughed. Steve collected their glasses and stood up. 'Did you mention to him what's been happening with Sophie... and also this Lewis thing?'

She nodded. 'But none of it registered. He's too involved with his own dramas to have room for any more. He said something like you'll manage to work it all out sis.' She stared out over the ocean towards the horizon, now hidden by darkness. 'That seems to be what everyone expects,' she pushed back her chair. Digger was immediately on his feet; tail wagging in anticipation of an evening meal.

Steve moved to put his arm around her shoulder. 'And you will.'

The three of them went inside out of the increasingly chill air.

'So now,' Steve had just said, 'let's leave all this,' he swept his hand over the remnants of the meal on the dining room table, 'until later. Lets sit down,' he gestured to the settee, 'and talk about Lewis.'

They had spent time happily pottering around in the kitchen, feeding the dog and making dinner together. Steve created a salad. Cathy grilled the marinated fish, all the while discussing Sophie; although about this split they were in agreement that they were glad it had happened. Jeff, they concurred was immature and Sophie didn't have time to be waiting around until he grew up.

'She needs to give up trying to save blokes from themselves and start to look out for her own interests,' Steve concluded.

'She can't change her nature,' Cathy was defensive. 'She's always wanted to help people. That's why she became a physio. You remember how she was as a little girl, bandaging her dolls, bringing home stray dogs.'

Steve nodded. 'That's okay in your professional life. But she can't get married to a stray dog. They don't make good husbands or fathers!' He smiled. 'There's a lot of men who'd like nothing more than to lean on a strong, supportive woman. You've seen the bra ads!'

'You missed out the bit about sexy.'

'That too!' he grinned. After some more thought he added. 'She'd do better looking for some

CHAPTER FOUR

one older than herself. A bloke with some experience of life.'

'But not a married man with two daughters,' Cathy responded quickly. 'You realise she is the same age as the one Tom's involved with, who is also childless and I'm pretty sure wants children herself.'

'He'd have to be mad to start that all over again,' Steve said with feeling.

They were finishing their meal as Cathy remarked, 'There's a lot to be said for arranged marriages.'

'Fat chance of that! Can you imagine how Sophie would react to us parading a line up of likely lads for her to choose from.'

'You make it sounds positively erotic,' she laughed and the phone rang.

'Let it ring through. It won't be important. Probably just someone trying to sell new mobile phone plan.'

It wasn't. It was Lewis, sounding distracted and somewhat irritated.

'I'm just coming down around the corner to your place. I can see the lights are on. So I hope you're there because...'

Cathy reached the phone and said hello.

'...Oh, you are, that's good. It's just that I have Sam with me...'

'...Hello Nana...' she heard a distant shout from the passenger seat.

'...And I was wondering if I could bring him in. Claudia has had to stay overnight in Melbourne unexpectedly on a job and I already had something planned for tonight.'

Within less that five minutes they were all greeting one another at the garden gate with Digger adding to the unruly melee, barking with excitement, attempting to lick Sam and at the same time to round them all up.

Sam struggled free of Cathy's welcoming embrace unwilling to be delayed from rummaging through his miniature backpack.

'Look at this Papa! He triumphantly held aloft his most recently acquired miniature car. Steve and he began discussing the finer details of the car's chrome-plated engine, with Sam pointing out the dual exhaust system.

'I won't come in Mum,' Lewis reached back through the gate,' and handed in a small bike. 'He can't go anywhere without this. I'm running late already.'

'I talked to Daisy Jacobs this morning,'

'Daisy?' Lewis paused and then, 'oh yes of course Daisy. How's her hip going?'

CHAPTER FOUR

He had already pecked a peremptory kiss on her forehead and latched the gate before she'd had time to say, 'Fine.' Then he was off down the path toward the cul-de-sac where he'd parked his car, calling out as he went, 'He doesn't need to be fed. He had an Egg McMuffin in the car. Give me a call tomorrow, when you've had enough of him and one of us'll pick him up.'

'I should have told him I'd already had enough of him, but that I'd never have enough of his son,' she muttered furiously when repeating all this to Steve. 'Egg McMuffin!'

'Who've you had enough of Nana?' Sam looked up from the precarious tower of Lego bricks he and Steve were constructing on the living room floor.

'Jane Howard.' She said the first name to come into her mind. 'Would you like a hot soy Milo with some honey in it?'

'Is Jane Howard a man?'

'Not quite. Oops watch out Digger. Oh, there it goes.' The tower was tumbled into ruins by the dog's tail.

The following two hours consisted of computer games, the completing of a largish jigsaw puzzle, a spelling lesson, a protracted and messy tooth cleaning session that seemed to involve far more spitting than brushing and a deep, over-foamed bath in which Sam spent most of time underwater wearing his snorkel and face mask, surfacing wildly enough to send water cascading almost to the door which caused Digger to yelp with wild joy.

As she was mopping up Cathy reflected on how she had managed with two children under two to also hold her career on track. And whether Deidre hadn't made the right decision after all. At least her two daughters were not showing any incipient signs of social maladjustment. Yet.

The three of them lay on Sam's bed, which he had triumphantly created all by himself from the sofa bed in the spare room, which was de facto Sam's room.

'I like my mummy's books better,' he crushingly informed them.

'Why's that?' asked Steve unfazed.

'Cos I know all the words in Mummy's books.'

'Well, these are all the same words, only in a different order,' Steve countered.

'Papa!' Sam rewarded his grandfather's quick wit by raising his eyebrows. He was beginning to appreciate Steve's line in humour.

With gritty determination he kept his drooping eyes open till page fourteen of *The Bugalugs Bum*

CHAPTER FOUR

Thief, then began to gently snore. As they eased away from him off the bed, he came wide-awake but didn't move, 'Leave Digger to sleep under my bed,' he ordered and returned immediately to a deep slumber.

They fell into their own bed shortly after, too worn out by the joys of grand-parenting to open up 'the Lewis thing' for discussion.

Cathy came awake in the middle of the night instantly aware that Steve, lying beside her, was wide-awake too.

'What is it? Did Sam call out?'

'No. No.'

Silence, except for the muffled sounds of the ocean.

'Then what is it? Are you alright.'

'Yes. Just thinking.'

'What about.'

'Roz Edwards called today.'

'Is Bob alright?'

'Yes. He's been given the all clear. For at least a year anyway.'

'That's good.' Cathy pulled the doona up a little. They always slept with the higher windows open so as to better hear the music of the ocean, but the nights were now cool.

'She called to say they've bought a camper wagon. They're taking off on an open-ended trip around Australia.' There was yearning in his voice. 'They're heading for the Gibb River Road.'

'Where on earth is that?'

'The Kimberleys.'

More silence.

'They're having a going away party next week and want us to come.'

'They're going that soon?'

'Yes. They don't want to put it off any longer. Its something they've always wanted to do. Bob's run in with cancer put it on hold for a while. So now they're going for it.'

'They'll miss their grandchildren.'

'Ummm.'

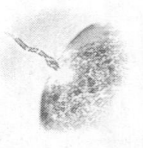

Five

Cycling to Coogee was the standard demand from Sam after a sleepover.

'I'll pick up the papers and stuff,' Steve told them, 'and collect you all at the far end of the beach with the wagon. We'll go on from there to brunch at Bronte.'

It was quite a distance for an almost five-year-old to cover on his bike, but Sam had become increasingly confident of his driving skills.

'Look at me!' he yelled as he careered ahead of Cathy along the wooden boardwalk which wound between the ti-tree scrub above the tumble of rocks through which the ocean hissed and surged.

Digger ran beside him, breathing hard through his mouth with the effort of keeping up.

As they came out of the scrub and up onto the parkland above Wylie's Pool she could see Sam waving and calling out to someone who returned his salutation from the far side of the grassy area, before he disappeared into the next clump of trees through which the way led down to the beach.

Cathy shielded her eyes against the light to see who was receiving her grandson's greeting.

'Oh damnation, she thought,' 'it's Daisy. There's no way I'm going to get into a conversation with her today.'

She gave a large full arm wave, made exaggerated gestures indicating she needed to quickly follow Sam and increased her walking pace till she was almost jogging.

'Who was that you waved to?' Cathy questioned when she managed to catch up with Sam and Digger almost halfway along the promenade.

'Umm? Who?' He frowned, not wanting to tear his attention away from a man who was using a long-handled, metal detector to scan the beach.

'Who did you wave and call out to back up there in the park? She pursued him.

'Oh,' he paused, still concentrating on the man, 'that was Ruby's Nana. What's that man doing?'

'How do you know Ruby?' she asked.

'What's he doing?' he insisted.

She told him, 'Looking for lost coins, or watches or whatever.'

CHAPTER FIVE

'Hey! Cool! Let's go and help him.'

'Samuel,' she used his full name to impress on him the importance of the question, 'how do you know Ruby. Please tell me.'

He was already bumping his bike down the semi-cycle of steps toward the beach. 'She's a friend of Claudia and Lewis...Mum and Dad,' he added in case she failed to grasp who he meant. 'She and Kit are getting married soon.' The bike fell into the sand.

'Kit?' Cathy managed to say in a weak voice.

'Yes. Kit's her girlfriend and they're getting married,' and he was tearing away across the sand toward the prospector, leaving Cathy to carry his vehicle.

The cafés overlooking Bronte beach were as crowded as always on the weekends. They waited a little while for a table at one in the middle, chosen because the woman who owned the shop used to be a teacher and Cathy had worked with her on several difficult Oppositional Defiance cases. The woman had been a brilliant teacher, but had become gradually so disillusioned by the lack of support from the Department and the amount of time she had to spend on paperwork and other non-teaching areas that she had chanced the regular salary and weighty lure of superannuation, to open up this café. It had been a high-risk gamble that had paid off handsomely. Her husband had also given up his career to join her. On weekends their teenaged children helped them.

Together they were riding the booming success wave of growth in the compact stretch of café society that catered for a growing niche market of affluent eastern suburbs thirty-somethings. These were the ones who found the Bondi scene a little too full of in-your-face singles and who used this row of cafés as a place to eat and socialise with friends in a home away from home atmosphere.

There was a lot of newspaper reading, numerous dogs under foot and almost as many infants, toddlers and small children who were there because of the playground and miniature train in the big park opposite. These were offspring of young couples, where both partners worked full-time outside the home and were glad, on Saturdays, to enjoy family time together.

From these eating places they could watch a dozen or so more hardy souls, protected by neoprene, slicing their surfboards across translucent green swells, which were made even more perfect this morning by a slight offshore breeze.

Cathy waved to her ex-colleague who was busy taking orders and serving behind the counter. The

CHAPTER FIVE

woman came out to their pavement table and they hugged in genuine pleasure.

'Don't let me take you away,' Cathy said. 'You're very busy.'

'No worries,' her friend smiled, 'always time for old compadres.' She shook hands with Steve and ruffled Sam's hair. 'What you got there, young man?' she leaned down to examine the small sandy pile Sam was ferreting through on the table in front of him.

'Treasures!' he looked up, his face a picture of pure pleasure.

'See!' He held up a single complex pendant earring of coloured stones. 'And look at these.' He rubbed sand off a couple of twenty-cent pieces. 'Old money.' He was about to lick the coins.

'Samuel! Don't do that,' Cathy restrained him. 'You don't know where they've been.'

'Yes I do! They've been in the sea for years and years. They were put there by robbers,' he announced dramatically rolling his eyes. 'They stole them from my house and I sent the Captain of the Dragons to get them back and told him to BURN THEIR BUMS OFF!'

His shout caused the two men in their early thirties, who were doing the Saturday paper's cryptic crossword together at the next table, to put down their coffees and glance at Sam somewhat disapprovingly. Cathy gave them a weak smile of apology and a conciliatory pat to their Jack Russell terrier, seated beside them, whom she thought looked embarrassed to be kitted out in a tartan polar fleece coat.

Cathy said, 'Actually he charmed them off a man who was scanning the high-tide line at Coogee.'

'Come with me, Sam,' the café owner offered, 'and I'll give you a big bowl of water you can wash all your treasures in.' When Cathy demurred with the comment that Sam mustn't take up her busy time, the woman smilingly insisted. 'I'm never too busy to have fun nowadays.'

'No regrets then,' Cathy asked, noticing how her ex-colleague appeared to be in blooming good health.

'None at all. We all work our butts off for the entire weekends but during the week we have time to surf and sail and read. I'm having a great life,' she laughed.

'You're very lucky,' Cathy responded.

'Yes. And like they say, the harder I work, the luckier I get,' she grinned.

Cathy told her. 'Things in the Department have only got worse. You're obviously doing well here and, even though it's not as secure, well, you've only got one life, so I guess I envy you. It was the right time to do it,'

CHAPTER FIVE

'The right time is when you know it in your heart. It really didn't have anything to do with the money. It was more that I just couldn't look in the mirror and imagine that woman still being there in twenty years, hanging in for the super. Now what would you like to eat?'

They ordered and she took Sam, carrying his treasures in a napkin, with her into the café kitchen.

As she attempted to pry one section free from the mammoth pile of the Saturday paper a collection of glossy, coloured, travel brochures fell out from where they had been concealed in the bowels of the newsprint. Steve bent suspiciously quickly to collect them up and began shuffling them back into a large plain envelope from which they had, obviously unexpectedly, revealed themselves.

'What are all those?' Cathy inquired.

'Just the stuff I told you I wanted to pick up on the way to collect you.' He made no move to take them out of their envelope or to pass it to her.

'But what are they?'

'Just some catalogues.'

'Travel catalogues?'

He nodded.

'On the Northern Territory?'

He nodded again and began to open the Metropolitan section of the newspaper.

'And the Gibb River Road?'

'Oh here's our waiter,' Steve appeared grateful to be excused from further explanations by the appearance of Sam striding out with a bowl of muesli topped with fresh fruit which he carefully placed in front of his grandmother.

'There you go Nana.'

The café owner followed with the rest of their order plus a plastic bowl containing Sam's treasures and the possibility of travel became lost in the necessity of ensuring breakfast was eaten and manners observed.

When they had finished, 'What do you say?' Sam asked Steve smugly as his grandfather said he would go in to pay the bill.

Steve obliged with, 'Please may I leave the table?'

Sam gave a gracious nod, also went in to say goodbye and when he came out still clutching the bowl assured Cathy, 'the lady said to keep it till next time.'

Cathy waved her thanks and goodbyes to her ex-colleague, still inundated with customers. They released Digger and the bike from the parked station-

CHAPTER FIVE

wagon and armed with a cricket bat and ball went down the little grassy wall into the ocean-side park.

There followed two hours of ball games, bike races, swings, slippery dips and rides on the miniature train during which time Sam was greeted by at least half a dozen friends from his kindergarten and Digger managed to sniff contemptuously at the tartan-coated Jack Russell whose owners had joined the parade which surged back and forth along the promenade front.

'There's that funny dog again,' Sam shouted, utterly unconcerned whether or not the men heard.

'He's not a dog,' Steve assured him. 'He's a farting dinosaur.'

'Papa!' Sam screamed with delight and rolled on the grass laughing.

On their way back through the narrow cutting, which sixty years before had been where the tram track had run but that was now used as an expensive parking lot, all fees going to help maintain the surf club, they came close to a posse of seagulls washing the salt off their feathers in a shallow run-off of fresh water. They rose en masse as Sam cycled up and he stopped to watch them soar out to sea.

As soon as Steve and Cathy caught up with him Sam was off again but within a couple of hundred metres he had stooped once more and they saw he was talking with two young women who had been walking down through the cutting towards him.

'He's a sociable lad,' Cathy remarked. 'I hope it doesn't get him into trouble.'

'Not with those two,' Steve said. 'They're your nieces.'

'Ohmygod,' Cathy muttered under her breath.

The family members exchanged hugs and a few pleasantries about the weather and work. Cathy avoided mentioning their father Tom, and hoped Steve would do the same. The sisters were so close in age, colouring, mannerisms and style of dress, which was fashionable but not extreme, they could have been twins.

They both exclaimed how much Sam had grown since they had last seen him and he insisted on showing them how he could cycle, wave one hand and whistle at the same time.

'Oh I'd love to have a little boy like him,' the older sister, Christabelle, said wistfully.

'You've got plenty of time,' Cathy reassured her.

'No she hasn't,' her sibling, Tanya, sounded certain. 'She's almost thirty.'

'I'm only 28.'

'Twenty-nine later this year.'

CHAPTER FIVE

'So there's time,' Cathy said soothingly and wanting to smooth the unequal contention between them she remarked to Tanya 'and you only have a year on her.'

'Yes. But I'm not having kids,' was the immediate and categorical response. 'I'm too selfish.' Tanya smiled in a self-congratulatory manner. Cathy found herself wondering how Tanya's mother Deidre would feel about that decision.

'Dad would love to have a grandson,' Christabelle added. 'He wanted Tanya to be a boy. But he got stuck with just two daughters and a wife.'

Cathy was grateful that Steve jumped in quickly to change the direction the conversation was headed.

'And where are you two going now. You're a long way from home aren't you? Can we give you a lift somewhere?'

'No thanks,' they both said.

'We did the cliff walk from Bondi,' this from Tanya. 'Its the only exercise we get all week.'

'And now we're on our way over to Ruby and Kit's place at Bondi Junction', Christabelle informed them. 'Its great that Lewis is going to help them have a baby,' she added.

AN IMMACULATE CONCEPTION

Cathy was having a phone conversation with her mother when Lewis came by to pick up Sam in the early afternoon. It was singularly unusual for her mother to phone her. Invariably it was the other way around; a regular Sunday early evening call to check in with Elizabeth, now eighty-four and living in a retirement complex of small town houses not far from Parliament House in Canberra.

Her mother sounded somehow different from usual. Hesitant? Frail? Cathy couldn't put her finger on it. She took the handset through to the bedroom to escape the raucous laughter of her grandson who was supposed to be having a siesta but was watching his favourite Wallace and Gromit DVD, *A Grand Day Out*

'Are you okay, Mum? Your voice is a little...' she searched for the right word.

' Croaky,' Elizabeth suggested and added, 'Perhaps its this flu I've had for a few weeks. I can't seem to shake it off.'

'I didn't know you had flu. You didn't tell me last week.' She hadn't meant it to sound so accusatory.

'The doctor said...'

So she's been to the doctor, Cathy thought, and she hasn't told me that either.

'... this year's flu shot is not quite as effective as it usually is.'

CHAPTER FIVE

There was a small silence during which Cathy sensed a feeling of disquiet.

'What about Steve and I come down to visit soon?' Cathy suggested. 'But I don't want you going to any trouble.' Elizabeth always insisted on providing luncheon for them. 'We could go for the smorgasbord at that hotel on the lake where we went for your eightieth.' She could hear her mother's breathing, but she didn't speak, so Cathy continued. 'Next weekend is out because Bob and Roz Edwards are having a farewell party. They're taking off to tour around Australia, but the following weekend...'

In a small, contained voice her mother said, 'I was hoping you could come this weekend.'

'But Mum its already 2 o'clock on Saturday,' she blurted out, then immediately regretted her words.

It was at this moment that she heard Lewis's voice call out from the garden and the scrabble of feet as Sam raced to greet him. Then, as her son bounded up the stairs two at a time, Steve called to her from the family room. She walked back through from the bedroom, with her fingers over the mouthpiece, but before she could speak, Lewis had pecked her on the forehead.

'Have to get Sam to a birthday party at Fox Studios,' whereupon Sam broke into a war whoop of excitement and was already halfway down the stairs, followed by his father, when he called back over his shoulder, 'Bye Nana. Bye Papa,' and following muffled words from his father, 'thanks for having me.'

She moved to the window and looked down on the three of them now clustered at the gate. She couldn't hear what was being said but for a second there was a freeze-frame image of them she would carry in her head forever, father, son, grandson, three generations and then the spell was broken and she spoke into the phone.

'Mum? You there?' No sound, but she knew she was. 'I'm sorry about that. Lewis rushed in to pick up Sam. They've gone now. And we'll leave straightaway. We should be there by just after six. I'll give you a call from the road.'

The fact that her mother didn't protest dispelled any doubts Cathy had about the necessity of an immediate visit.

'Steve doesn't need to come down,' her mother suggested. Cathy picked up immediately on the intimation that she would like to see her daughter alone.

'I'll see how he feels but whatever he decides, I'll see you soon. I love you Mum,' and she said her goodbyes.

Steve decided to come with her, as she had hoped he would.

CHAPTER FIVE

'I like the drive down there,' he assured her. 'And,' he added, ' it will hopefully give us time for some quiet conversation. Just the two of us.'

Six

'So just how are they going to make this baby?' Steve's voice sounded harsh.

Hundreds upon hundreds of eucalypts passed the windows of their comfortable four-wheel drive. Cathy sat beside her husband as they drove through the thin winter sunshine and wondered if someone, somewhere... some eccentric boffin in some half-forgotten university research lab, was busy calculating just how many eucalypts there were growing all over Australia. All over the world come to that. Holding together dry soils in Spain, Southern California, North Africa. China. Australia's greatest gift to the world. A metaphor for....

'How?' Steve's repeated question broke into her reverie. She knew herself well enough to know she was playing mind games in an attempt to avoid examining the issues.

'I'm more interested in why?'

'Let's get the how out of the way first.'

She shrugged her shoulders. 'I have no idea.'

'Are they going to make love?'

'I shouldn't think so, as it wouldn't be love.'

'Are they going to go to some hospital or clinic and do it all medically?'

Again she shrugged her shoulders.

'Or are they going to do it on their own with Lewis jerking off and this girl jamming his sperm up there with a turkey baster?'

'STEVE!' she shuddered. 'For god's sake! Do you have to be so crude?'

'Well, that's how they do it. Its no good being prissy and pretending its a bloody immaculate conception.' He gripped the wheel and she realised how distressed he was. Probably this whole thing was even more difficult for him, as a long-lapsed Catholic, than it was for her as a luke-warm Protestant.

'How d'you know about that?

'The Immaculate Conception?' he tried to joke, 'it's in the Bible. His hands relaxed a little. 'The other stuff I read up on the Web.'

'The Web!' she was incredulous.

'You can learn about anything on the Web. From how to build your own nuclear suitcase bomb

CHAPTER SIX

to...turkey basters.' He sighed. 'I find I'm not happy with the idea.'

'Which particular idea?' she asked quietly. 'Lewis donating his sperm, our grandchild being raised by a lesbian couple, or the turkey baster?'

'All of the above and more.'

'Me too,' she reached over and squeezed his thigh.

They passed the off-ramp to Bowral. The last time they'd driven down to Canberra this area had been thick with choking smoke from huge bush fires but now the blackened limbs were sprouting vibrant, green, new life.

'Should we just be glad,' she suggested, ' there will be another new piece of our genetic material out there. Lewis and Claudia seem perfectly happy to just have one child and Sophie's still a bit high risk at this stage so perhaps this is the only other shot we'll get at immortality.'

'Does that mean,' he asked, 'you think any child, no matter what its circumstances, is better than no child?'

'My head thinks that,' she replied, 'but my heart tells me otherwise. We may very well all be playthings of the gods, but do we have the right to treat our children as playthings? Creatures to be created for our own pleasure.'

'Isn't that the reason we had Lewis and Sophie?'

'That was lust!' she squeezed harder. They both laughed and were quiet for while, then she asked, 'what are you thinking about?'

'That wet afternoon in Dubrovnik ...'

'Wet enough and cold enough to dampen even the excessive enthusiasm of that newly graduated architecture student,' she teased him, 'who was determined to spend his November honeymoon inspecting every Renaissance villa and cobble-stoned alleyway of the old town,'

'...so he took his rager of a new wife back to their room in the former convent overlooking the Dalmation coast and fucked her brains out.'

They laughed again as she added,

'And Lewis was created!'

Steve nodded.

She went on, 'I remember telling old Doctor Davidson that I also knew when we made Sophie, though we were more sedate by then.'

'Sedate enough for the sand dunes at Palm Beach, with Lewis asleep in the back seat of the old Kombi.' He licked his lips and tried a leer.

She laughed, 'I gave him a sanitized version, just mentioning the full February moon. He looked at me over his half-glasses and said, 'a nice romantic

CHAPTER SIX

idea my dear but I'm afraid not medically possible' but then what would he know...'

'...he's only a man!' Steve finished her story and they both smiled.

They were quiet again for a while, immersing themselves in the Shostakovich First Symphony, which was being played on Classic FM.

When it came to its perfect ending, she remarked, 'we're very fortunate,'

He nodded in comfortable agreement.

'We loved each other and we had two great children. It seemed simple at the time. Maybe these two women love each other. But it's not so simple for them. Maybe they will be great parents. Does the fact that they are the same sex disqualify them from being good parents? I have no idea what the stats are on lesbian couples breaking up, but they surely can't be any higher than the almost fifty percent divorce rate of heterosexual couples. Perhaps having a baby would give them a focus and a reason to try to stay together.'

'You keep working at it Cathy and you might just manage to persuade yourself. And why the past tense for we loved each other and had two great children?'

'You know I still love you. More, even. But the children aren't children anymore. I love them both of course. But you know what? I'm having trouble liking Lewis. He takes us for granted.'

'So he should. That's what parents are for. To be there when you need them, not when you don't. We're like muzak. Irritating when it's turned up too loud.'

'Very clever,' she snapped.

'And true,' he retorted.

After she'd been quiet a while he asked, 'Not sulking are you?'

'I'm pissed off that he didn't tell me. Doesn't he care what I might think? Do I have no say in all this? Apart from anything else its bloody bad manners. He just rushes in and out. There's never time for a proper conversation about anything important.'

'You always told me,' Steve chuckled, 'that I should tell you if you started to sound like your mother. Well, you're starting to sound like your mother!'

Cathy felt suddenly tired. She rubbed her fists into her eyes and stared through the windscreen at the continually unfolding highway.

'It is bad manners though' Steve agreed. 'Still maybe he didn't tell us because he realised we would have all the reservations we are now expressing. But no, we don't have any say in it. He sees it as his and Claudia's decision alone. I doubt he has even consid-

CHAPTER SIX

ered what Sam might think in years to come. For whatever reasons they don't anticipate any of the complexities which make us fearful. I've got to take a leak.'

Seated on the bright green, hard plastic seats under the harsh neon lights of the roadside service station café, Cathy thought Steve looked drained and offered to take over the driving.

Steve demurred, 'I like to drive. It gives me an illusion of control!'

They drank their coffee and immediately regretted it. They shared a sugary donut to take away the bitter taste and regretted it even more. Back in the wagon the conversation resumed.

'Is it our age? Are we turning into boring old farts?' she asked.

'Yes, it is our age. But with that comes experience and hopefully with all that some wisdom.'

'And fear.'

He nodded. 'Afraid so. Inevitable really. And I think that's what a lot of this emotion is about. Fear. The 'what ifs'. What if the child is born with complications? What if it gets really sick at some time? What if they can't afford what we would consider adequate housing, health care, education? What if the mothers split up? Does Lewis just provide the sperm and walk away? Where does his responsibility begin and end. Where do our responsibilities begin and end.'

The highway curved gently left and they began the long approach, through the avenue of winter bare poplars to the shallow waters of Lake George. 'I'll never think of you as an old fart,' he said gently. The shadows lengthened as the evening drew in. They were close to Canberra now.

'I feel so small-hearted,' she swallowed hard. 'Everyone else seems so genuinely pleased. Sophie. Tom's girls.'

'They don't have children so they don't know that fear.'

'Daisy.'

'Anything just so long as she gets to be a great-grandmother.'

'Tom.'

'Too busy, as you so kindly pointed out, with his dick, to be thinking clearly. And I promise you that certainly not everyone, not everyone by a long, long way is going to take to the idea with gusto. This is going to separate the wheat from the chaff. We're really going to find out who our friends are.'

'Life has taken a sudden lurch,' her voice was tremulous.

CHAPTER SIX

Last week it seemed so simple and straightforward. I feel as though I have stepped off into the deep end.'

'Just keep treading water and ring your Mum.'

Elizabeth Stuart greeted her daughter in her usually reserved manner; but the fleeting embrace told Cathy that her mother was even thinner than she had always registered her as being, the light kiss revealed an even cooler than remembered skin and was it her imagination or was her mother's always punctiliously erect posture slightly stooped?

The two women exchanged pleasantries; each knowing that beneath this surface, socially acceptable charade, each was scanning the other for deeper truths.

Elizabeth had the drinks tray set ready to pour her own whiskey over ice and for her daughter; she raised the bottle, 'Gin and tonic?' Cathy nodded her acceptance. 'You must need this after your long drive.'

'Steve did the driving,' and responding to her mother's look of inquiry, Cathy explained, 'I dropped him off at the motel around the corner. He sends his love of course, but he has some paperwork to get on top of,' Cathy had a sudden flash memory of the Northern Territory and West Australian travel brochures, 'and the drive down was a good way of finding time alone together to talk.'

'To talk about anything in particular?'

She never misses a trick, Cathy thought and replied, 'Not really. Just life, death and the whole damn thing.'

Elizabeth nodded and repeated quietly, 'Life, death and the whole damn thing.'

They sipped their drinks. Cathy felt the warm glow created by the gin spread gently though her system and her body relax.

'Well I'm glad he's come down because there's something heavy I want to move.' She smiled. 'Men have their uses.'

'What heavy thing is that Mum?'

'The big bookcase in the den. I've taken the books out to make it lighter and you know it comes apart into two halves, top and bottom but it was too heavy for Mrs. Driscoll and me to move on our own.'

Mrs. Driscoll titled herself Administrator of the Residents' Community Centre, a bustling self-important woman who was almost as wide as she was tall and Cathy shook her head at the improbable picture of her tall elegant mother and this woman struggling to move the large antique bookcase.

'Mum!' she exclaimed. 'You shouldn't be trying to move heavy furniture, with or without Mrs. Driscoll. Isn't there a man employed by the centre for just that purpose?

CHAPTER SIX

'Yes. Billy. But he's such a gossip.'

Deciding not to pursue that remark Cathy instead asked, 'Where do you want to shift the bookcase to?'

'I don't want to shift it. I just want to pull it out so as to get a packet out from behind it.'

'A packet of what? Did it fall off the top and slip down behind?'

'No. It's a packet I stored there when I first moved in fifteen years ago. I didn't want it to get lost but I didn't want to be tripping over it all the time.'

'So you hid it there.'

Elizabeth said nothing.

'What's in this packet that is important enough for you to risk being crushed to death by a toppling bookcase? And what are you going to do with it when you get it out.'

Elizabeth poured them both another drink, adding ice with tongs from a small elegant silver plated bucket. Like all the furniture and accessories in her mother's home, this piece was something with which Cathy had grown up and therefore had hardly registered as anything more than just another part of the jigsaw puzzle of childhood.

'Its your father's Commission, his medals, his cap, his Sam Brown belt and the flag that was placed on his coffin for his funeral,' her mother said. 'I want you to have them.'

'Heavy duty shit,' was Steve's response when she told him of her mother's revelation. They were lying in bed in the hotel where they had taken to staying when visiting Elizabeth so as to minimise the impingement on the domestic situation of an octogenarian widow.

'How did you respond to that?'

'Naturally I asked her, why now? I mean she does look a bit more frail. But not like she's going to die. Not tomorrow anyway. Or anytime soon. You know what a private a person she is, but I think the two gins helped me and I managed to ask her if she was worried about her state of health, or whether she wanted to go for a medical check up.'

'And?'

'She said no, that she knew her body better than any doctor, that all she was suffering from was punctuated equilibrium.'

'What the hell is that?'

'Its a gap in the fossil record.'

'Is she loosing the plot?'

'Not at all. It's her dry wit. Her academic mind. That's what happens when you spend a lifetime studying and teaching palaeontology. I didn't get a full

CHAPTER SIX

handle on it, but it goes something like this; every now and again, at seemingly fairly regular intervals of something approaching two or three hundred thousand years, there's a blip in the fossil record. It's running along smoothly and it comes to a sudden stop and then it appears to do a leap and pop up again at a different level. You follow?'

'Sort of'

'Well you know how we've talked about looking in the mirror one day and feeling you've aged five years?'

'Frightening.'

'Then it trundles along at that level for a while before seemingly doing another big deterioration. That's punctuated equilibrium at a human level, or anyway that's Mum's theory and her way of accepting her own ageing.'

'And?'

'She's just done a blip.'

'I see. And how did it go once you had agreed on that diagnosis?'

'She said she wanted to hand over Dad's stuff to me for safe keeping, because I am the eldest and because Tom is, in her words, 'a bit of a rascal.' I didn't ask her if she knew of his most recent rascally behaviour. Then we retreated to generalities and she served her usual asparagus quiche. Did you have something to eat?'

'Yes. I had a pizza delivered, drank the beer from the room fridge and watched the game on telly. Boys will be boys!'

She snuggled up to him. 'Was it a good game? '

'The really good stuff came at the very end when the second rower bulldozed his way through the defence and scored a try, an equaliser, with only forty seconds to the whistle. The crowd went totally crazy. Especially when one of the Maroons gave them the finger and mouthed off at them.'

'All good clean fun. Great example for young boys. No wonder we have problems in our schools.'

'Hey, lighten up.' He put his arm under her shoulders and pulled her closer.

Later as they were slipping into sleep she asked, 'Did you bring those Northern Territory and Kimberley brochures with you?'

'Yes,' his voice though sleepy was still wary.

'I'd like to look through them tomorrow.'

Seven

'You don't need to open that up here,' her mother's voice had an anxious edge, as she proffered the largish, brown packet to Cathy.

Steve gingerly edged his way backwards from behind the bookcase, which he had managed, with a little balancing support from his wife, to ease out a sufficient distance from the wall to be able to rassle forth the piece of family history.

Cathy fingered the heavy string and read the carefully written words; 'The contents of this packet are bequeathed to my daughter Catherine Stuart and my son Thomas Stuart or to their heirs. It was dated fifteen years previously and signed in her mother's strong hand.

'Open it when you are home. You and Tom must decide between you who keeps what. Little boys love medals and he has only daughters. I would just like to think it would all stay in the family.' When Cathy remained statue-still her mother continued; 'Why don't you lock it in your car and then we can help Steve put all this back in its place.'

It took a couple of hours to recreate the perfection Elizabeth required. The beautiful jarrah wood glass-fronted bookcase was home to her honed down library of reference and specialist volumes on palaeontology, collected over a professional life spanning four decades. Pride of place was reserved for a first edition of On The Origin of Species, which had been presented to her by the Australian National University when she retired from her professorship.

In the capacious cupboard, which made up the lower part of the piece, were stored manuscripts, articles, magazines, which her mother had either contributed to or written in their entirety. These had been placed in neat and perfect chronological sequence.

'All this has been donated to the university library,' Elizabeth stood back and surveyed their handiwork. Cathy and Steve, on their knees in front of the now tightly packed lower cupboard, exchanged glances. Both knew the other one was thinking, 'well why the hell are we doing their packing for them?'

As if reading their minds, Elizabeth offered praise. 'Thank you, you've done a great job. Now its all

CHAPTER SEVEN

in order for them.' She smiled with satisfaction. 'Let's have a little congratulatory drink and do what you suggested on the phone Catherine, have a late luncheon at that place overlooking the lake. It's a perfect day for it.'

Indeed it was and Cathy thought Walter Burley Griffin himself would have agreed that it showed off his eponymous lake to perfection. She had seized the only remaining empty window-side table; spreading sweater and handbag around to lay claim and then settled herself into a chair. Her mother and Steve had gone off to raid the long and amply supplied buffet table promising to bring her back a plate of choice food.

She always enjoyed visiting Canberra. It was a return to the womb and as such, comforting. There were whole new suburbs now, but all she knew about them was that they had names such as Amaroo, Banks and Ngunnawal.

Her Canberra had hardly changed. There were the somewhat incongruous white arches of Civic and the gracious old Canberra Hotel There were the wide streets of Deakin and Forrest, lined with large deciduous trees and thick high hedges behind which were big homes with well-tended lawns and luxurious gardens overflowing with gardenias, azaleas and hydrangeas. The atmosphere had remained very polite and well mannered.

She enjoyed going to the top of Red Hill, though it seemed more of a hillock now than the full-blown mountain of childhood memories, to look down on the new Parliament House, built on ground where she had romped and played with friends from kindergarten. She felt she had an inkling of the Aboriginal concept of belonging to and being part of the land. This was her Dreaming.

She liked to walk by the substantial house in Melbourne Avenue where she and Tom had lived with her widowed mother and maternal grandparents. The big tree was still there in the front garden, the one in which the two of them had built a tree house and from which he had fallen, broken his arm and caused much consternation to his over-protective mother and grandmother. Poor Tom; accident-prone from childhood, always seeking and receiving the suffocating attention of females.

She hadn't been conscious of being fatherless. How could you understand what you were missing when you'd barely had it? Thomas Samuel Stuart, was part precious name, part myth. It wasn't until she had seen Steve interacting with their own two children that she began to have a sense of loss. But you

CHAPTER SEVEN

couldn't change the past. All you could do was go on into the future.

That, she realised, was what her mother had decided to do. No good weeping, wailing and gnashing your teeth at the unfairness of becoming a young pregnant widow with a toddler. People felt sorry for you, for a short while, then they got on with their lives and expected you to do the same. Elizabeth had moved back in with her parents, attended university and recreated herself as an independent professional woman. Not much time for romance and not much choice, what with Canberra's population being a mere 30,000.

She had vague memories of her mother having one or two male friends during her early years. But by the time she was attending the Girls Grammar School, her own life was so full that ...

'What are you thinking about?' Her mother's question broke into her reverie. 'Life, death and the whole damn thing?' She never forgot even a passing comment.

Steve placed in front of her a plate piled with prawns, marinated octopus, salmon, dipping sauces, salad, tabouli, stuffed vine leaves, hummus. 'I can't possibly eat all that,' she wailed.

'Don't worry. I'll eat what you can't manage.' He put down his own equally overfilled plate. 'I'll go

87

and get some bread and wine. Red or white Elizabeth?'

'He looks after you well,' her mother remarked as Steve hurried away. 'You're very fortunate.' She looked down at her own abstemious meal. 'He's an enthusiast.'

They ate slowly, savouring the view over the lake, with its intermittent fringe of impressive government buildings, which was so central to the atmosphere of the capital city and as well the plate of curiously mixed cuisines, redolent of its multinational community.

The restaurant was crowded with lunching families many of them seemingly from the various embassies and consulates. Clichéd national characteristics were very apparent. Big tables filled with parents and children. Once they had supervised their children's meals, the adults swapped places, leaving tablefuls of youngsters to devour cakes and ice cream while they joined together in seemingly jovial discussions over coffee.

'International relations look pretty easy here,' Steve commented, back with his plate of seconds.

'Sunday family lunch, its a great tradition,' Cathy sounded wistful and caught her mother's perceptive glance.

'How is your family?' she asked.

CHAPTER SEVEN

'They're fine,' she heard Steve respond, but her mother kept her gaze directed straight at her and raised her eyebrows in silent inquiry.

Cathy drew in a breath.

'Coffee anyone?' Steve stood up from his chair.

'Steve doesn't want to worry me,' Elizabeth said still looking directly at her daughter. 'But I would rather know. I find the unknown far more distressing. Imagination is the killer.'

Steve sat back down.

Cathy looked at Steve, then back to her mother. 'Tom is having a fling with a thirty-three year old. Sophie has kicked her boyfriend out and...' she hesitated, lowered her eyes and then brought them back up to face her mother's questioning expression, '...and Lewis is planning on fathering a child for a lesbian couple. And he didn't even tell us himself.'

Her mother's face creased into a wide smile of relief.

'Is that all! From the way you look I thought one or other of them had been diagnosed with a terminal disease. That's always been my greatest fear,' she nodded in agreement with herself. 'Death should have the decency to take us in age order. What do you think?'

'I think you're amazing,' Steve stood up again, 'and now I'll get those coffees.'

Cathy remained silent.

Elizabeth, still smiling with relief, said, 'Tom has always had flings.'

Astonished, Cathy asked, 'How do you know that?'

'He tells me about them,' and ignoring Cathy's look of amazement, 'and the ones he doesn't tell me about I guess at. I can tell just by his tone of voice over the phone. He's so transparent. His ego is so fragile, he needs these little adulteries to be bolstered up. I was at fault. I over-indulged him as a small child and when he grew into a good-looking young man he looked so like his father I think I was a little bit in love with him. For some years I felt so guilty, felt that I had ruined his life by loving him too much. But I came to realise that people ruin their own lives. Its a matter of choice and I chose to give up guilt.'

Steve returned with their coffees.

'Mum knows about Tom,' Cathy informed him. He didn't look too surprised.

'He'll drop her when she starts to make demands.' Elizabeth stated.

'At thirty-three she'll be wanting to have babies.' Cathy suggested.

'Then he'll run back to Deidre, who'll make him pay with another diamond ring or holiday in Italy.'

She sipped her coffee. 'Sophie's made a sensi-

CHAPTER SEVEN

ble decision so the chances are she'll go on making them....'

'And Lewis?' Cathy asked, amazed to be having this personal conversation with her mother. 'How do you feel about your great-grandchild being parented by lesbians?'

Elizabeth Stuart looked out across Lake Burley Griffin. 'There have been a lot of changes in my lifetime, not all of them for the better. I'm glad I won't be here to see what the next generation make of their world. I don't feel I've learnt much in all the years but perhaps there's one thing I have.'

She was speaking very softly and Cathy and Steve had to strain to catch her words. 'You have to let go of your children. You will always love them, but you may well stop liking them and if you don't cut the ties and let them free, you will never be happy.'

They thought she had finished speaking but she went on looking across the lake and continued.

'I didn't want you to marry Steve,' they glanced at each other, 'because I knew he would want to try his luck in Sydney... that you would make your home and family there and I wanted to keep you close to me. I was nursing my mother at home at the time and later my father, so I had to stay put. Then Tom wanted to follow you and I reluctantly agreed.' There was another long pause. 'By the time mother and father were dead I had my career established here and it seemed too late to try to break into the Sydney academic world.'

'What I experienced with them made me determined never to become a burden on my own children.' Cathy wanted to reassure her, but Elizabeth kept talking. 'I plan to keep my independence and make decisions about my own life for as long as possible'

'Children are not purposely cruel to their parents, just unthinking, and self-absorbed. You've kept in touch. Phone calls. Visits... when it suited you. The same with Tom. But its not how I had dreamed it would be. I too would have liked to be surrounded by my family at regular Sunday lunches.'

It was late afternoon by the time they dropped Elizabeth back at her townhouse and they had decided to stay another night. They declined her offer of a cup of tea.

'We won't come in Mum. We'll make an early night of it so we can get going at sun-up. That way I need only take a flexi half-day and Steve can rearrange his own work schedule. Oh, and we mustn't forget to phone the neighbours and let them know, so they'll feed Digger and take him for a walk.'

CHAPTER SEVEN

'I'm very glad you came down Catherine. Thank you for responding so quickly.' Her mother's embrace was fuller than Cathy could ever recall it being, though again she registered her mother's frail frame. 'You too Steve,' she said with genuine warmth. 'Take care of each other.'

Usually, after saying her goodbyes, she turned and went inside before they had driven off. This time she waited at Cathy's side of the vehicle while they put on their belts and started up. Cathy let down her window.

Elizabeth said, 'I would like, if there's time, to come up to Sydney.' It was as if this was a considered decision that she had just made. 'I would like to see everyone. Have a family gathering. Could you organise that?'

'Of course. I'd love to.' Cathy told her.

Her mother nodded.

'When would you like to come up?'

'Sooner rather than later. I think that would be best. You have the Edwards' farewell this coming weekend.' Again Cathy marvelled at her mother's attentiveness and memory. 'So what about the weekend after that? A family luncheon for the whole clan.'

The two women smiled at each other.

They spent the early evening looking through the travel brochures of Northern Australia and it quickly became obvious to Cathy that her husband had quite a good handle on the general geography of the area; place names and distances. When she questioned him about this he told her; 'it's something I've been thinking about for a while and I've looked it up...'

'On the Web.' they said simultaneously and laughed.

'The font of all information,' Cathy went on, 'from turkey basters to Turkey Creek. But why have you been looking it up? Are you really thinking we should follow in the Edwards' footsteps?'

'Its something I think we should seriously consider, taking off for a year. We could rent the house. Take Digger of course and just shoot through.' He looked positively exhilarated by the idea.

'What about your practice? Your clients are not going to want to put off building their dream home for a year while their architect goes walkabout.'

He glanced down at the vivid photographs of grand gorges, pristine waterfalls, wetlands and space and said with fervour, 'I've had it with all those eastern suburbs dream homes. I don't want one more conversation about granite versus composite stone bench tops, shabby chic versus distressed retro, what

CHAPTER SEVEN

colour glass splash-back for the kitchen, hingeless or semi-hinged glass shower doors, or what shape the bloody drawer handles are.'

They were both silent. On the page between them beckoned an ochre Bradshaw pre-Aboriginal figure, still vibrant after at least 60,000 years of dancing on the wall of an overhang, near a cave mouth four thousand kilometres to the north, on the edge of the vast continent.

In a quieter tone he added, 'It will all still be here when we get back. I can pick up the threads and if that fails I'm certain I'll be able to find freelance work with one or other of the big architectural firms. They've offered me work in the past.' He paused. 'But if we don't go, I know I will regret it. I feel it in my bones. Though that might just be arthritis,' he attempted humour.

'What about my job?' she asked quietly.

He was blunt. 'Do you still feel like a Crusader or is it just the super?'

'Bit of both, ' she admitted to herself for the first time, 'sometimes more of one sometimes more of the other.'

'Well if its the Crusader I reckon we could both do some of that in some other way. And if it's the super, I know I won't be lying on my deathbed worrying about whether I made enough money. What I don't want is to be lying there worrying about not having swum in the Mitchell Falls.'

There was another silence before Steve added, 'we're not getting any younger and I want to do that trip while I have all my faculties and good health to enjoy it.'

Cathy was cleaning her teeth in preparation for bed when she remembered she had left her mother's packet under the front seat of the wagon. Despite already being in bed, Steve said he would go out to the parking lot to bring it inside. 'You'd have to put all your clothes back on. It's brass monkeys out there.'

'Thank you. You're my champion! But I wouldn't sleep well with irrational fears of it being stolen.'

'Me neither.'

Steve was away so long that Cathy was beginning to be anxious and when he did finally return he looked so shaken she feared her anxieties were well founded.

'Where have you been?' she asked as he sat beside her on the bed, turning the packet over and over in his hands. 'Are you alright?'

'I ran into Billy in the lobby.'

'The handyman from Mum's place?'

CHAPTER SEVEN

Steve nodded. 'He'd obviously been having a drink in the bar. He asked me how long we were down for and if we'd seen your Mum yet. Then he wanted to know how she looked to us because he was concerned about her.'

Cathy encouraged him to continue. 'He told me that on Friday she asked him to drive her to the funeral home. On the way there he asked her whose funeral she was attending and she told him, 'my own. I want to choose the music and pay for my own coffin and flowers.' He went in and waited for her. And that's what she did.'

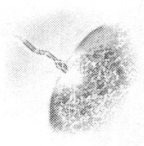

Eight

'Forty-four is hardly young,' Doctor Davidson had said to Cathy more than a decade previously. 'Some women begin their menopause in their mid thirties, and with your history,' he peered down through his half-glasses at the clutch of file cards on which the medical nature of her entire adult life was charted in indecipherable shorthand, 'its hardly surprising.' His remark had been a turning point for her.

'I've been through two pregnancies and fifteen annual pap smears with that man,' Cathy growled to Steve later. 'Over the years he has referred me on to various other specialists, all of them men, who have performed a termination, a tubal ligation, three operations for the removal of ovarian cysts and another two for the removal of fibroids.' She sounded overwrought.

'Let's not forget the Delightful Drama of the IUD,' Steve announced in a theatrical voice designed to lighten her mood. 'The Saturday night when you haemorrhaged all over the floor of the hospital emergency ward frightening the knockers off the assorted car accident victims and damaged drunks and causing the poor medical student in charge to all but faint!'

Cathy was not to be deterred. 'No more men. I've had enough of them running around my insides, telling me what they know I should feel and think. Remember when I told Doctor Davidson that when I menstruated I could feel which one of my ovaries was ovulating and his response was to send me to a psychiatrist. They've made careers and fortunes out of women like me. That psychiatrist wrote an international bestseller about women and their bodies. The obstetrician who delivered Lewis was knighted.'

'Not because he delivered Lewis,' Steve managed to squeeze in. 'And then he was de-knighted.'

'The one who popped the cysts and chopped the fibroids went on to get an OA '

Steve went to speak but Cathy glared at him. 'So I say no more men.'

'Am I man enough for that to include me?'

Cathy burst into floods of hormonal tears but a week later, after spending hours in conversations with

CHAPTER EIGHT

friends and colleagues and on the phone she managed to track down a female gynaecologist who agreed to take her as a client.

'I'm first and foremost a fertility specialist,' Doctor Sandra Forbes had explained to her, 'which means I am mostly involved with issues at the other end of a woman's cycle but I know how difficult it is to find a woman in this field so I'd be happy to take you on.'

Over the years of Cathy's annual visits they had built up an easy rapport. The clinic, in an inner-western, semi-industrial suburb was always busy but Doctor Forbes never made her feel hurried. While she took blood, checked Cathy's breasts, examined her internally and took a cervical scrape, the two women talked about their children; Sandra had a teenaged boy and girl, their husbands; Sandra's was an obstetrician, and recent political issues which, on the last regular annual visit during the previous week, had included stem cell research and Australia's falling birth rate.

There was an easy female affinity, which made Cathy feel comfortable and natural in taking off her clothes and giving over her genitalia for exploration. She had started taking hormone replacements, which had immediately lessened the moody blues, drenching sweats and extreme fatigue. Dr. Forbes had explained at length the possible long-term negatives of the treatment but a relieved Cathy had assured her that, 'if it takes five years off my life it will be worth it just to feel more human than I've ever felt.'

So it was with no trepidation that when they arrived back home from Canberra she responded to the phone message from the clinic, which had been left on their home phone earlier that morning. She thought vaguely that Sandra Forbes might want to discuss educational issues because she had hinted that her son was showing signs of not being happy at his school.

The drive back up from Canberra, in the growing early morning light, had given her and Steve time to talk about Elizabeth's visit to the funeral home.

'Its nothing to panic over,' Steve tried to reassure her. 'Remember what she said yesterday about liking to be prepared...'

'Not being a burden on her children...'

'And wanting to keep her independence and make decisions about her life for as long as possible. Well this is in keeping with that idea.'

'I can't not tell her that we know...'

CHAPTER EIGHT

'Perhaps wait until she comes up to visit. That's not long.'

'And I wonder what she really thinks about this Lewis thing.' Cathy pondered. Every conversation they had now seemed tinged with 'this Lewis thing'.

'Well, you got the feeling that she was not over-enamoured with the idea, but that what else is there to do but just roll with the blows. She is after all one more generation removed and at her age I can understand feeling rather distant from the hurly-burly angst of modern life. A detached calm.'

'Is that what you're aiming for,' her voice expressed the slight irritation she felt at his tone.

Unfazed he replied, 'Long-term yes, but I have other, intervening short-term goals.'

Images of the Mitchell Falls danced between them.

There was a slight pause after the clinic receptionist answered her call and she gave her name, then Dr. Forbes herself came on the line.

'Good morning Cathy,' her voice sounded professional and reassuring.

'Hello Sandra. Sorry it took a while for me to get back to you. Steve and I needed to make an unexpected visit to my mother in Canberra and we stayed longer than planned.'

'Everything alright I hope?' Dr. Forbes asked perceptively.

'Well, you know, she's not getting younger. How is it with your family? Jason hanging in there?

'Sort of. But I wanted to get in touch with you because I need you to come back in. The results of last week's pap smear are not as conclusive as I would like them to be and I need to do it again.'

'That's fine. I'll make another appointment.'

'I'd like to see you as soon as possible. Today.'

Cathy didn't properly hear the rest of what Dr. Forbes said. It became a blur of 'nothing to be anxious about', 'new laboratory testing procedures' and 'better to be safe', all made to sound faraway and indistinct by a loud, drowning roar. Part of Cathy's brain registered that the sound was her own racing pulse.

She put down the handset, having somehow managed to say that she needed to go into her office briefly, but that she would come over to the surgery later on that afternoon. She could hear her own voice making these arrangements but it was a disembodied voice, which felt remote from her.

She was still standing by the phone when Steve came through from his office at the back of the house accompanied by Digger, who had been so pleased to see them and so determined that they were not going

CHAPTER EIGHT

off without him again, that he would not leave Steve's side.

Steve had a sheaf of papers and brochures in his hands and rolls of plans under his arms. He was talking, but she couldn't quite make sense of his remarks either. It was if there was suddenly a wall of glass between her and the rest of the world that made for a sense of distance and detachment. Added to which, everything seemed very slightly out of focus... blurry and unreal.

He kissed her cheek. 'Gotta go. Running late for the builder and that will never do. Builders think all architects are self aggrandising jerks and being late only just feeds their theory.' He gave her another kiss and noticing that she seemed distracted, he added, 'don't go on worrying about Lewis. I'll phone him today and make a time for us to see him and Claudia to have a talk about it all.' Then he was out the door, shadowed by Digger.

'She's power-hungry.' Pat tortured her ballpoint pen as she sat on the other side of Cathy's desk.

In a haze of disconnectedness Cathy had managed to get herself to her office. The traffic had seemed to be travelling at great speed. She heard voices and singing coming from a great distance and it took some time for her to realise that it was the ABC's afternoon radio host chatting with a visiting Canadian singer. After negotiating her way from the car park, past the commissionaire, through the open plan office to her room, she was still standing looking out of the window at the winter-bare plane trees lining the street when her colleague Pat, who had followed her in without knocking, closed the door behind her. With no preliminaries she informed Cathy that Jane Howard had formally applied for the Assistant Director's job, in which Cathy had been acting for the past eight months.

'She's power-hungry,' she repeated, 'and a crafty wheeler-dealer.'

The depth of venom in Pat's voice and the angry expression on her face was sufficient to penetrate the cocoon in which Cathy had felt enclosed. There was a release of tension.

'She says such nice things about you,' Cathy teased her friend.

Pat rolled her eyes.

Cathy continued, 'and nowadays wheeler-dealers are admired as being excellent networkers, while being power-hungry is considered by the market place to be appropriate behaviour. The expression 'The eater, eating is eaten' comes to mind.'

CHAPTER EIGHT

Pat peered at her across the desk as if fearing to find that her long-time friend and colleague had been indulging in a secret tipple. Still unsure, she retorted rather sharply that 'Buddhist philosophy is not an appropriate response anymore than it was to suddenly take an unrequested long weekend, just as we're coming into the home stretch before the deciding interviews for the job.'

'Jane Howard,' Pat fairly spat the name out, 'made damn sure that everyone from the commissionaire to the Director knew that you had taken an early mark on Friday and then compounded it by taking Monday morning off as well. She's fed the spiteful rumour mill with ideas that you no longer have the stamina for the job.

'Perhaps she's right.'

'What!?' Pat fairly exploded. 'Only a few days ago we were planning our campaign strategy for making sure you stay in the job.'

'A few days ago, I was a different woman,' Cathy smiled a little sadly. She looked down and began to roll the intertwined white gold and platinum wedding ring Steve had designed and had made for her. Pat waited but with barely controlled impatience and irritation. 'I was in good health, a happily married career-minded woman, almost at the top of her profession, in a successful marriage with a happy daughter, a settled son and daughter-in-law, an erratic but charmingly likeable brother, a distant but loved mother, and a grandson who filled me with joy.

She let go of the ring and looked Pat in the face. 'Today,' she paused and repeated, 'today my grandson still fills me with joy. Steve wants to give up his architectural practice and go walkabout on an open-ended trip around Australia. Sophie has given her long-term boyfriend the heave-ho . My brother is considering running off with a young woman and starting another family. My mother is preparing to die. And Lewis is going to become a sperm donor to a lesbian couple.'

Pat's eyebrows shot up. 'Phew!' and after a short silence, 'and I just thought you were taking a sicky!'

'I might be taking a few more of those too. Starting with this afternoon. There seems to be some irregularity with the results of the pap smear I had done last week. The gynaecologist wants me to have it done again as soon as possible. Irregularity being another catch-all like 'appropriate'.'

'Aaah.' Pat nodded. 'So that's the nub of it. The sound of angels' wings. Intimations of your own mortality.'

'Perhaps. I certainly felt a big shift in perspective, which surprised me. But I think it's an accumula-

CHAPTER EIGHT

tion of all the other emotional hits. Especially this Lewis thing.'

'Children,' Pat sounded suddenly weary. 'Just when you think its safe to get on with your own life.'

Cathy knew Pat was thinking about her own son. Three years ago Pat's husband took what was euphemistically called, early retirement. He received a considerable payout and with an eye to their future, they had sold their large home in the leafy north shore suburb of Warrawee, where they had raised their family of two daughters, both now married, one with two children of her own and a longed-for son. With these funds they had bought a sizeable acreage in the Hunter Valley. The plan had been to develop a vineyard and they both worked hard to achieve this goal. They attended viticulture classes, read and studied the science and as well developed a comprehensive knowledge about local land formations and weather conditions.

They lived in simple rustic style on the property and did the initial, tough, hands-on heavy work while, in order to keep at least one regular salary going, during this period of their steep learning curve, Pat continued working at the Department. During the week she bedded down in the small flat they had bought in the Chinatown of Chatswood. Every Friday night she hotfooted it to the Hunter, returning to her solitary state on Sunday evenings. It had been a period of challenging change and adjustment as well as learning. Cathy had often expressed her admiration to her friend for their determination and just, as Pat put it, 'when we saw the light at the end of the tunnel, it turned out to be a goods train.'

Their twenty-two year old son, on holiday in Bali, had an horrific accident on a hired motorbike. Barely clinging to life he was airlifted back to North Shore Hospital, where he spent three months, first in intensive care and after that under-going a succession of massive operations. He was released from hospital in a wheelchair. 'Thank god,' Pat told her, 'there is no brain damage. No spinal injuries.'

But there was also no use of his right arm, where the musculature had been completely destroyed and for many months to come, he had only a very confined use of his right leg, the shattered bones of which had required complicated pinning and return visits to the hospital for operations as well as daily physiotherapy. The long-term prognosis was uncertain, but Pat and Les knew that their son would never again be the strong, athletic, happy-go-lucky young man he'd been, on the very verge of springing off into a life of his own. The even darker psychological impact was unthinkable.

CHAPTER EIGHT

After an initial period of adjustment to the change in their responsibilities, Les had gone back up to the vineyard because nature didn't make concessions for the vagaries of family life and there were things that had to be done, otherwise all the hard work they had put in would come to nought. Pat had soldiered on, somehow managing to continue her work schedule, as well as cooking nourishing meals for her son and organising his physiotherapy visits. His ex-girlfriend came back on the scene and, along with some of his close mates; they started to re-engage him in normal life. Everyone accepted that it would be a long time before he would feel strong enough to fly the nest again.

During this period the two women became closer than ever. Cathy had been a substantial support and without anything being said, they both recognised that the time had come for that support to be reciprocated.

'Why has Lewis decided to do this?' Pat asked.

'I don't know. We haven't had a chance to talk yet.'

'How do you feel about it?'

'Not happy.' Cathy sighed. 'To be honest, not at all happy. The idea of my grandchild being raised...' her voiced trailed away.

'By lesbians.'

Cathy nodded. 'How do you think you would feel?'

'I can't imagine. I gave up trying to imagine how I would feel in hypothetical situations ever since I had my tubes tied.'

Cathy looked puzzled.

'Because six months before I had it done... this was years ago... I had met a woman at a party who told me she'd just had her tubes tied and felt free for the first time in her life. And I was shocked and told her so. I went on about destroying her womanhood, that she was a victim of male domination and that her husband should have had a vasectomy instead.'

Pat shook her head. 'My god, what judgmental arrogance! But the kick to the story is that six months later when I became pregnant while I was still on the pill... and having three children under four at the time, I was so distraught that my doctor suggested I consider having a termination. I did, and just to make sure, I had my tubes tied at the same time.' She laughed. 'And that woman was right. I did feel free and what's more, I didn't feel any less of a woman. So I learnt that if you haven't been there, you can't really know. But I do feel for you.'

Cathy smiled. 'You're a good woman Pat.'

CHAPTER EIGHT

'And you know Jilly,' she referred to her older daughter, 'is so upset about not falling pregnant, especially since her sister had her second one, that she and Ahmed are seriously considering going to a clinic for help. Of course they couldn't tell his family because it's against their religion. As if it all wasn't difficult enough already.'

'Lewis isn't going to a clinic. It's going to be a handyman job.' Cathy stopped short, aghast at her choice of words. Then both women burst out laughing.

Then Pat said, 'See what I mean about making it as hard as possible.'

Now it was the double entendre that made them laugh.

'We have to keep laughing,' Pat said. 'Let's just hope these girls have a sense of humour.'

'God yes,' Cathy agreed emphatically. 'It would be too awful if they are the lesbian equivalents of Germaine Greer!'

'You don't know them?'

'No. Everybody else seems to. Tom's girls do.'

They talked for a few minutes about Tom's latest peccadillo and both agreed that he needed to grow up.

'Or Deidre should put bromide in his tea,' Pat suggested.

'And Sam knows them. He tells me they are getting married.'

Pat asked 'Is that legal?'

'I don't know. Recently I've found I don't know much about quite a few things.'

They touched briefly on Steve's restlessness and Elizabeth's funeral plans before coming back to Cathy's questionable health.

'No good worrying before you have all the facts about what you're dealing with,' Pat tried to reassure her. 'So I think you should go over to your doctor straight away. You won't be able to do anything here. You'll not be able to concentrate.'

'I wanted to go through the figures Claude Borsellino asked me to look at on Friday.'

'I'll do that.' Pat brushed aside her objections. 'I'll write up a little report to satisfy him and I'll even forge your signature on it.' She laughed. 'Remember when we used to practice our own and each other's signatures in school? I bet I can still do a good Catherine Stuart! She stood up. 'But one good turn deserves another right?'

Cathy nodded.

CHAPTER EIGHT

'Not a whisper about possibly not putting yourself forward for the job. I want Jane Howard to sweat all the way to the finish line. So mum's the word.'

'Mum is the word,' Cathy promised, 'and Grand mum. Like I said, you're a good woman and a good friend.'

'Yes, well don't go getting all soppy on me. Because I don't fancy you!'

'Nor me you.'

Nine

Women, the title of the quarto-sized book caught Cathy's eye. She picked it up from the low table. Photographs by Annie Leibovitz, words by Susan Sontag. In her febrile state she couldn't take in the words but she sat in the calming atmosphere of Dr. Forbes blue-painted waiting room and turned the pages, looking at the black and white photographs, which celebrated women.

Women of all ages, sizes and colour; brilliantly exposed in their most secret moments. Some of them famous; Hilary Rodham Clinton working on her papers on a verandah of the White House, actor Elizabeth Taylor with her small dog, philanthropist Brooke Astor in a truly elegant black and white outfit and model Jerry Hall breast feeding her son Gabriel. Some of them high achievers; a Lieutenant General in her uniform, a research scientist beside a pickled

AN IMMACULATE CONCEPTION

brain, and the former Chief of the Cherokee Nation. There were sex entrepreneurs, coal miners, trapeze artists, musicians, sculptors, dancers, opera singers, a baseball pitcher, a rabbinical student, a maid, a drag car racer and members of the Crips all girl gang. Inspirational portraits of women in life and the life force in women.

On the other side of the room a couple in their mid to late thirties sat clutching at each others hands, deep in an obviously troubled conversation. Even though they kept their voices low, Cathy could hear they were speaking Italian. They were both dressed top to toe in elegant black and both had luxuriant dark hair, hers a tumbling mass of curls and his a gleaming gelled perfection. The woman began to cry quietly.

The door to Dr. Forbes' inner office opened and two smiling women in their early thirties emerged, thanked the doctor and strode briskly out through the waiting room chatting in an animated manner.

Dr. Forbes gestured for Cathy to come on through but Cathy hesitated, signalling toward the Italian couple who had been there before her. The doctor motioned that it was okay and Cathy gave a small smile of encouragement to the crying woman as

CHAPTER NINE

she followed Sandra into her room where the two women shook hands.

'Heavy stuff,' Cathy grimaced.

The doctor nodded in agreement. 'Joy, fear, anger, grief. We experience plenty of emotions in here.'

Suddenly Cathy let out a small cry, 'Oh no!' and gestured at the wall behind Sandra's desk. 'Not you too! Its a conspiracy!'

Startled, Sandra turned to look at the photograph hanging on the wall in pride of place, which Cathy had moved across to examine more closely.

'You don't like it? I had it put up over the weekend.'

The colour photograph, more than a metre wide, showed in close up a tumble of smooth round boulders squatting on the edge of a vast area of undulating dry spinifex country. In the very distance was a flat-topped mesa. All this soft purpley-green geographical splendour was set under a crystalline blue cloudless sky. There was a sense of limitless horizons.

'And what d'you mean, a conspiracy? Sandra asked.

'Steve is trying to get me to give up work and go walkabout with him. He's collecting brochures and travel catalogues full of photographs of places just like that. ' She studied the photograph. 'He says that if he doesn't go, when he's lying on his death bed, he'll regret it.'

'I chose it because the rocks look pregnant and because it's called *Women's Dreaming*,' Sandra told her.

Both women smiled and Cathy said, 'you see what I mean. It's a conspiracy!'

Sandra opened a manila folder on the desk in front of her and Cathy felt her slip from being Sandra into being Dr. Forbes. There was a slight pause as both women adjusted to their roles. Doctor. Client.

'So,' Dr. Forbes looked up and met Cathy's steady gaze. 'The biopsy of the pap smear we took last week shows some changes in the cells.'

She hesitated and Cathy said in a tone of voice which was calmer than she felt, 'I need to know all you can tell me. Please don't hold back because you fear I may not be able to handle the truth.'

'Good,' Dr. Forbes responded. 'First of all I need to do a colposcopy, which is like a regular pap smear only I take a larger sample and send this off to the pathology lab. The best outcome would be to find

CHAPTER NINE

that the changed cells have not broken the surface of the cervix. In that case we can settle for a scrape. If the changed cells have broken the surface or if they have affected more than fifteen percent of the cervix... and this can be determined by performing a cone biopsy, then there is still a good chance the affected cells can be excised. If the affected area is any larger then it will be necessary to remove the cervix.'

'Is this cancer? Cathy was surprised at how steadily she asked the question.

'Until we get the results of a new biopsy I can't give a definitive yes or no to that. Again the best outcome would be for these changes to be precancerous. You have a lot of plus factors.' the doctor smiled. 'Your general health is good. Exceptionally good. You have no underlying medical problems. No heart, vascular or lung disease. Your family history is good.'

Cathy recalled the silver framed photograph of her dead father which showed him in his army uniform and which her mother kept on the top of a corner cabinet in her bedroom. She had a passing thought too of the parcel containing his badges, cap and burial flag, which just this morning she had carefully put away in the drawer under her bed.

'You don't smoke.' Dr. Forbes was saying. 'You drink in moderation. You eat well. You are not overweight. You work at staying healthy and you exercise regularly. But...'

'I'm in my late fifties.'

'And that's the negative,' the doctor agreed.

'The immune system is running down.'

Dr. Forbes nodded.

'What are the stats on life expectancy for women who have their cervix removed due to cancer?' Cathy wanted to know.

'I can pull out the figures for you. But even without the exact figures I can assure you that there a lot of women out there literally running around without a cervix.' They both smiled at the mental picture this conjured up. 'This is most definitely not a death sentence Cathy.' Having imparted the hard medical facts Dr. Forbes became familiar again. 'Now lets get this colposcopy done.' They went through into the examination room.

She lay on her back, naked from the waist down, with her legs spread wide, feet resting in metal stirrups while Dr. Forbes held her vagina open with a hollow metal insert and scraped at the head of her cervix with a speculum, Cathy always managed the physical discomfort of the experience by envisioning

CHAPTER NINE

herself swimming. It was an old yoga practice she had perfected over the years and which she had used to great effect in a range of unpleasant situations.

The water was like cool silk, which rippled from her shoulders down her back and along her legs. In the light that shafted through the surface she could see the tiny little hairs on her arms as she stroked through the water which parted willingly to let her glide through.

'All done,' Cathy heard Dr. Forbes say and she came back to where she was lying on the bed. 'That's good. You can get dressed now.' Cathy began to re-don the well-cut navy pants suit and red shirt which she had worn to give herself the boost she had needed to face first her office and then this appointment. Sandra, still with her back to her as she processed the sample in readiness for the testing laboratory, commented, 'I'm glad you said you want to hear the truth as we go through this together. I find we get better outcomes for women who ask for the truth.'

'I've never been any good at pretending.' Cathy zipped up her ankle boots which added eight centimetres to her height and immeasurably to her self-confidence, 'and I loathe secrets. Especially,' she said with vehemence, 'family secrets.' She stood up, shaking down her trouser legs as she did so, settling herself into her clothes while Sandra Forbes turned to face her with a look of sympathetic inquiry. 'Lewis is donating his sperm to a lesbian couple. He didn't tell me. I found out from the mother-to-be's grandmother.'

'And you're not happy about that.' It was more a statement than a question. Cathy shook her head. 'With the mother being a lesbian or the fact that Lewis didn't tell you himself?'

'Both. We haven't talked with Lewis about it yet. We only just heard on Friday and since then there's been a lot of stuff happening.'

'Your mother?'

'Yes. And now this.' She gestured at the sample in Sandra's rubber gloved hands.

'Let's go back into my room.'

Back seated under *Women's Dreaming*, Sandra asked, 'Why do you think Lewis should have told you?'

'Because...because I'll be that child's grandmother. Doesn't that count for anything?'

'No.' Sandra Forbes was emphatic. 'You say you want truth. That's the truth. There are a lot of other people in the line to be counted before it gets to you. Hard truth. But truth. You're a generation removed from the choices and obligations involved. You had

CHAPTER NINE

your chances, with Lewis and with Sophie. Now they have their chances to make the most of their lives and perhaps Lewis sees this as one way of doing just that.'

'He's not doing it through a clinic.' The moment the words were out of her mouth Cathy realised it sounded as though she was trying to enlist Sandra's support for her antagonism by pointing out that they would not be using Sandra's or any of her fellow gynaecologist's professional skills.

Sandra didn't comment or look up from her notes and Cathy sensed an unexpected reserve. When she did speak it was to say, 'Home inseminations are more popular in the gay than in the straight world. The method is more acceptable in their culture. Perhaps because they feel they are already outside the mainstream, so creating life this way is less of a leap to make. I could tell you about the pluses in trying to do it this way.'

She waited for Cathy to say in a small voice, 'please do,' before continuing. 'The major plus for the women is that the donor is known to them. Another plus is that the procedure takes place in a non-medical setting, most usually in a safe, friendly quite often loving, caring, supportive home environment.'

'And the negatives?' Cathy asked quietly.

Sandra told her, 'As with much in life, the major plus turns out to also be the major negative because, even assuming the donor is well known to the would-be mother, the fact that there is no medical screening is definitely a downside. Very hard to ask a friend who is volunteering to father your child when he was last tested for HIV or Hep-C. It doesn't take much imagination to realise how much high emotion there is around all this.'

Cathy nodded in understanding.

'Quite often the donor is a bisexual or homosexual friend of the lesbian couple and then of course it is even more important that he is medically screened. You talk about family secrets,' Sandra went on, 'how many happily married women remain ignorant for years of the fact that their husband is bisexual and lives a dual life.'

Instinctively Cathy thought of Steve and then Lewis and frowned in objection at such an idea.

'It happens,' Sandra insisted, 'a lot more often than you would imagine. People's sexuality is very complex. Similarly the reasons a man donates his sperm are often also complex.

'Another downside of home inseminations,' she went on, 'is the absence of specialised counselling; that is counselling by someone who is very familiar

CHAPTER NINE

with the issues that invariably arise for same sex parents.'

'Such as?' Cathy felt she had stepped into a minefield.

'Seemingly simple points, such as what details go on the birth certificate. Under the law as it is at the moment the birth mother is the legal guardian of the child. If it is stated on the certificate that the father is Unknown, then the donor has no legal rights such as access to the child. Sometimes that's what a home insemination donor wants, paternity at a distance and that's what the women parents want. A no strings donor. But I have seen it happen that as the time of the childbirth comes closer, the man changes his mind and wants to be registered as the legal father with all the rights to which that entitles him. Under a loose, ad hoc arrangement these problems can become very significant. There's less chance of these issues getting out of hand if they are thoroughly aired in a pre-insemination counselling session. All donors we use here at the clinic sign a legal form saying that they would be happy to meet the child if and when the child wishes to do that.'

The light on *Womens Dreaming* had softened, so that the colours had deepened as Sandra said, 'It's also important in a same sex couple that they decide between them who is to be the principle care-giver.'

'The mother,' Cathy reacted instinctively.

'No, its not always the birth mother,' Sandra countered. 'Sometimes the partner who most desires to have a child is unable to do so for medical reasons, the same sort of medical reasons which can make it impossible for some straight married or single women to bear a child. Its important to talk all this through beforehand because if the two women do split up then the birth mother, the one registered as the mother on the birth certificate, is the legal mother and it can happen, just as it does in heterosexual relationships, that the child is used as an emotional pawn between the two parents.'

Cathy found that she had been holding her breath and she now let it go.

Sandra smiled at her and said, 'but though I do believe experienced outside counselling is important, I should tell you that by far the vast majority of lesbian couples we assist into motherhood in this clinic come through that door far better prepared for parenting than their heterosexual equivalents. That's true.' She gave a little laugh. 'I am often in awe of them. They mostly have been planning and working towards parenthood as a goal for some time. They have good jobs, they've paid off their car and they are paying off their own home. They know exactly what their financial situation is right down to the cost of

CHAPTER NINE

water rates. They've done their overseas travelling and they are ready to make the sacrifices parenthood demands. They've got the nursery ready and they know where they want the child to go to school. What's more, about a third of same sex couples we see here bring their own donor. It's truly impressive.'

Sandra stopped speaking and then asked, 'Do you want to hear all this?' Cathy nodded and Sandra told her,

'I am more than happy for them to bring their own donor...' Cathy noticed that Sandra paused as if making room for her to respond. But when she didn't, Sandra continued, '...and there's a good reason for that, because although there has not been any study done, I have an uncomfortable feeling that the present donor pool is too small. And that could pose problems.'

'Why's that? Cathy asked.

'Unknown consanguinity is the medical term for it. A small donor pool means that one man's semen may be used to fertilize numerous women. Which is not so much of a problem in the broader spread of the IVF community, but the gay community is still pretty tight and it is possible that twenty or so years down the track the offspring of same sex couples may meet and marry, with unfortunate results.'

Sandra's face brightened, 'But there again, the gay community are ahead of the crowd. They take the trouble to become as well informed as possible, so quite often they specifically raise this possible problem and ask that their donor not be used in any other attempted pregnancy.'

'Gay women,' Sandra continued, ' are also mostly younger than the single women we treat who have left it until their late thirties to decide to go it alone, mostly in the hope that the right partner was going to turn up. Younger too than the straight couples, quite often because most of them are in second marriages and want children with the new partner or, increasingly, because they were busy having what they saw as a good time and they put off having children until it was more or less too late.'

'There is one other downside to home insemination,' Sandra said, 'and its probably the one which finally floors all but the most determined. Fatigue.' She smiled again. 'Humans, being what we are, give up fairly quickly. There aren't too many Leyton Hewitts out there. Success depends to some degree on several inseminations being attempted over a period of only a few days. And if fertilization doesn't occur within a few cycles, in other words within a few months, the strain on all the inter-relationships, between the two women and, in this situation

CHAPTER NINE

between Lewis and his wife and also between the two women and Lewis and his wife can be tough enough for one or other of them to want to drop out.'

'The figures say it all. If you have a hundred heterosexual couples using an IVF procedure to become pregnant, half of them will do so within three months, seventy-five percent within six months and eighty-five percent within a year. Lesbian couples using the home insemination method have only a fifteen percent success rate.'

For a while the two women scrutinised each other's faces. Sandra, calm and experienced. Cathy, bewildered and overwhelmed asked, 'Why?'

Sandra spread her hands wide, silently asking why what?

'Why do they want children?'

Sandra appeared affronted. She focused intently on her client, a woman she thought she knew and said, 'for all the same reasons as you and I wanted children. To begin with, because they are women.'

Cathy went to speak, but Sandra, anticipating what she would say, continued, 'Just because they are in a relationship with another woman does not diminish in any way, or to any degree, the overwhelming desire they have to become a mother. They are driven by the same natural imperatives as the rest of us. I would even go as far as to say that at some deep level they are even more driven.'

Women's Dreaming filled the wall above Sandra's head. In the closing afternoon light the frame seemed to disappear into the wall leaving just the splendid scene. It was as if the two women were actually sitting in the shelter of the great boulders conducting women's business.

'They love each other and as a natural expression of that love they want to create a family together. Perhaps even more than straight couples they want to have the opportunity for a new start.' Sandra checked herself, appearing uncertain whether or not to expand on this line of thought. Searching Cathy's expression, she nodded as if giving herself permission and continued.

'Its far from unusual for the birth mother in a same-sex relationship to have experienced some form or other of sexual or physical abuse.' She gave Cathy time to register that information. 'This abuse has generally made her wary if not actually frightened of becoming close to men. With another woman, she feels safe, nurtured. Quite often that woman to the outside, straight, conventional world appears to be the man in the relationship. She has more than likely not had sexual relations with a man. She has always felt attracted to and more comfortable with people of

CHAPTER NINE

her own sex. Together they want the opportunity to raise a family. And like all parents they are determined they are going to make a better job of it than their own parents did. It's the dream we all have when we have children. Why should they be denied that dream?'

Cathy felt hot tears well up. She blinked them back. 'I'm ashamed of my feelings. They were immediate, instinctive. I've never thought of myself as prejudiced. I have gay colleagues, we have gay friends.'

'But it's different when they are the parents of your grandchild.'

'Yes. It is. I can't lie about how I feel.'

'Perhaps not, but you can work on changing how you feel,' Sandra said as she passed a box of tissues across the desk. Cathy had a fleeting thought about how many boxes of tissues must get used up on tears in this office. Tears of grief, loss and acceptance but also tears of hope and achievement. Sandra continued, 'and that would be a positive way to move forward. This baby, like all babies, all children, will need as much love as it can get. It may help you to make these changes if you know there's lots of literature which supports the fact that two women make just as good parents as woman and man parents. There is no literature to support the idea that they do not do as well. And,' she gave a significant pause so as to make sure Cathy was really listening, 'there's also no literature which indicates that having same sex parents, either two women or two men, alters or interferes with the child's sexuality in any way at all. They may be a little more adventurous than the crowd. Rather more willing to take risks in life.' She was silent for a while before saying, 'But their only real problem is societal prejudice.'

Cathy scrunched the tissue into a ball and rolled it between her hands. 'What if this child needs special care, or help with education, or...if the women separate? I'd feel some responsibility...' her voice trailed off.

'These are issues which Lewis and his wife and the two women should be discussing. They may welcome input from you and Steve. They may not. You'll have to assess that. But I'd say that it's a good start that you feel a sense of responsibility. We should all show more responsibility for every other human being, not just for our grandchildren.'

'Do you know the commonly accepted lowest estimated figure for child abuse is ten percent. Ten percent of all children are abused. At the present moment the Child Abuse Hotline is funded to three hundred thousand dollars a year and,' she stopped again to ensure Cathy was listening, 'private funding

CHAPTER NINE

provides all those monies. Not a cent from the government. This lack of public funding means that a child desperate enough to call in has only a fifty percent chance of getting through to help. And that in a society which likes to consider itself child friendly. The government needs to put its money where its mouth is and spend less time trying to make political capital out of a few hundred lesbians a year who want to have babies.

'As for a society in which there is a more than forty percent divorce rate,' Sandra shook her head, 'don't even get me started. I'll just say that if I were the Dictator of Australia, in divorce settlements I would always award the house to the children. Instead of the children being shunted around between Mum and Dad's places I would make the parents move in and out of the children's home. One week it would be Mum living there, one week it would be Dad. It would be the parents who would have to pack their suitcase and bring their toys and bike. It would be the parents who would suffer the ignominy and desperate feelings of insecurity.'

'So if, Cathy,' Sandra smiled to lessen the heat which had been in her voice, 'these women do separate, then your sense of responsibility, your love for this grandchild, will be even more required. I'm sure you tried to instil in Lewis the values you and

AN IMMACULATE CONCEPTION

Steve believe in yourselves.' Cathy nodded. 'Well, working from those values, somewhere along the line he developed the idea that helping two women to become parents was, in human terms, a good thing to do. You supported Lewis as a child, through his school, into his career, into his marriage and parenthood. Now it would seem to me to be a good idea to support him in this decision too. Its not like he's taken to dealing in drugs or juggling the company accounts. Perhaps you could work on being proud of his decision. And Claudia's too no doubt.'

'After that,' her smile broadened, 'you could even work on getting to know the women. They could become extended family. You never know, you might even like them. One thing I do know, for sure, you'll love the new grandchild, because that's the way you are. Try to embrace the challenge. Approach it with a positive, open heart. Enjoy it. We none of us know how long we have to enjoy life.' She looked down at Cathy's medical record. 'We all live in fearsome times.'

The two women were silent for some time before Cathy said, 'Thankyou,' adding, 'I've taken up a lot of your time on something which has nothing to do with my own health and I really appreciate your advice.'

CHAPTER NINE

They stood up and as Sandra came out from behind her desk, they spontaneously embraced. 'That's fine,' Sandra said, 'We're all in this together and anytime you want to talk about it I'm here. And I'll be in touch with you as soon as we have the results of the new biopsy.'

'Oh yes, of course, thankyou, I'd sort of forgotten about it.'

'Well there you go,' Sandra teased, 'there's one positive thing to come out of it already!'

The waiting room was empty, the Italian couple gone. A double spread of the Annie Leibovitz photographs lay open on the small table.

'That's a terrific book,' Cathy gestured towards it.

'Indeed,' Sandra agreed. 'It was given to me by a lesbian couple who we assisted into parenthood.' She picked it up, turned back to the inside cover and passed it to Cathy to read the handwritten inscription.

A huge thankyou to Sandra Forbes and her magnificent team for helping us make our dream come true.

Outside, in her car, Cathy sat quietly for a time thinking through their conversation and mulling over Sandra's parting words, 'We're all in this together.' Was there something she had missed? She turned on

AN IMMACULATE CONCEPTION

her mobile phone. The message alarm rang immediately. She checked and found that Steve had rung six times asking, in increasingly frantic tones, where she was and what time she would be home because he had arranged a dinner with Lewis and Claudia for that evening.

Ten

Wylie's water swallowed her up. Cold. She set out to cover the full length of the pool underwater but came up well short of the sea wall, gasping for air. Turning onto her back and kicking to reach the edge, she lay her forearms along the rough top surface and rested her chin on them to stare out at the heaving ocean. The surging wave crests beyond the wall were illuminated by the rising moon. Dark came so early in mid-winter.

Behind her, security lamps lit the wooden deck above. There was no one else in the pool and she knew it was highly unlikely that anyone would come to share her wild swim. She slipped out of her bathers and tied them tightly by their straps around her waist. Free. She felt the water enter her body. Cleansed.

It was high tide and the waves came in sets of increasing height until the last couple broke across the wall into the pool. She held on and waited with anticipation, emptying her mind of the day's news, events and emotions.

Here all that registered was the cold of the water, the taste of salt, the hissing and roaring sound and movement of the ocean. Mere human dramas didn't count one jot. It didn't matter whether you were gay or straight, whether or not you had cancer, whether you got the top job or even whether your mother died.

The first of the waves to breach the wall carried with it some rubbery strips of kelp torn from the ocean floor. She dove under the surface, holding her breath, resisting the tumbling motion of the water. Surfacing, she could see the next wave just off the rocks, travelling toward the pool wall at speed. She gulped in a lungful of air and aimed downwards, letting the water plunge on top of her, churning her naked body just above the rocky floor.

Then, as she broke the surface, the hissing ocean fell back over the wall leaving her gasping and laughing. For a while longer she played in the waves. Then, emptied and revitalised, she left the ocean to its solitary game.

By the time the maitre d' showed them to their window seats, looking out across the forecourt of the

CHAPTER TEN

Opera House toward the great white sails, Steve was willing to be slightly mollified by the fact that although they were running almost five minutes late, Lewis and Claudia had not yet arrived. Cathy decided against making light of this because she knew how much he loathed being late. Inexcusable rudeness was how he described it, and he had only just managed to subdue his irritation with Cathy when she had arrived home, wrapped in the salt encrusted beach towel she kept in the boot of the car for occasions when she felt the sudden need for a swim.

'Where the hell have you been?' he had burst out at her as she ran in from her car. He jumped up from the sofa and followed her through their bedroom and into the bathroom, accompanied by a tail-wagging Digger. He looked very cross. 'I have been phoning you all afternoon.' She stepped into the shower. Above the hiss of the blissfully warming water she heard him raise his voice to be heard.

'Did you get my messages? We're having dinner with Lewis and Claudia in three quarters of an hour at that bloody expensive place on the Quay. It was their choice. God knows why.'

Cathy quickly fingered the shampoo through her hair, rinsed it and massaged in some conditioner. As she soaped up and rinsed off, Steve continued a barrage of questions without waiting for any answers. So wound up, that he talked without pausing for breath.

'Why didn't you ring me? Last time I saw you, you looked so down in the mouth I thought I'd better get this Lewis thing sorted out as soon as possible. I spent god knows how much time chasing both Lewis and Claudia around on their bloody mobile phones, leaving messages and finally getting through to her and more or less having to insist that we meet them tonight. She had to try to arrange a baby-sitter and said she would call back and never did and then finally Lewis called to say it was all on and that we should meet them down there at the Quay and, before I could suggest some place else he said he was glad to be meeting up because, get this, he has some good news he wants to share with us. Good news! Digger stop that at once!'

Cathy came out of the shower in time to see Digger with his head down the toilet bowl drinking clean water from the pan, his paws balancing on the seat. This curious behaviour pattern, which Digger had displayed ever since he had been big enough to reach down into the pan, had always quite amused both Steve and Cathy, even though they actively discouraged it by keeping the toilet lid closed and by reminding Digger that he had his own constantly re-

CHAPTER TEN

plenished bowl of water by the back door. But right now Steve was not in the mood to be amused by anything. Although, Cathy thought, it was only ever Steve who forgot to lower the seat.

He came into the bedroom with her where, following his jacket and tie lead, she put on a discreet, grey beaded camisole top with a matching jacket and black Chinese brocade trousers. She slipped on high-heeled grey beaded sandals, attached the antique pearl drop earrings he had given her for their twenty-fifth anniversary to her earlobes, put a smudge of colour on her lips and a wipe of mascara on her eyelashes. All the while Steve talked, a sure sign that he was very agitated.

'And throughout all this I tried to contact you. I checked with your office. Jane Howard answered your line and said no one knew where you were. I left message after message on your mobile. And when you finally turn up here, what do I find, you've been for a swim! A swim! In the dark! In mid-winter! Have you gone mad, or what?!'

She turned to face him. 'I'm ready to go now. I'll use my hair-dryer in the car. We'll still make it on time.' She smiled at him. ' I'm sorry to have worried you. You look very handsome and I love you.'

Watching him now as he scanned the drinks menu, she thought again how much she loved him, that he was indeed a handsome man and more than that a loving, compassionate, intelligent man and that she was a very fortunate woman, despite the duff hand life had dealt her this past week.

The maitre d' seated another couple at the window table next to theirs. Cathy covertly observed the restaurant's rituals, noticing that every single one of the waiters had a shaven head, though all of them were twenty-something and that the slim, dark-haired, energetic maitre d' sported a perfectly manicured little zif, a discreet earring in both ears and a fabulously expensive watch. He looked far better groomed and more elegant than most of the patrons and she found herself wondering how much he earned and if he planned to make a career of hosting well-heeled diners in improbably stunning settings.

Steve had just asked her, 'I'm dying for a drink. D'you think we need to wait for them?' when she saw Claudia and Lewis arrive at the top of the stairs and the maitre d' fall upon them with what looked for all the world like genuine affection. They chatted animatedly as they wound their way through the tables towards them and Cathy noted, almost as if for the first time, what a good-looking couple Lewis and Claudia were, the disparity in their heights, she small-

CHAPTER TEN

boned and petite, he tall and gangly-limbed, made them appear perfectly matched. Her lustrous mass of natural honey-blonde hair shone in the subdued lighting and when Lewis held Cathy by the shoulders to kiss her on both cheeks she felt how large and strong his hands were. The family welcomes over, Lewis gestured toward the maitre d', 'Mum and Dad, this is Carter. He runs the show here.'

There was much friendly banter during which Carter apologised for not having recognised Steve and Cathy as Lewis's parents when they arrived. 'But I am looking forward to getting to know you both much better,' he positively beamed at them. 'I think this is an occasion which calls for champagne,' he announced, 'I have just the right one,' and bustled away.

Cathy caught Steve's eye and they exchanged a circumspect look of anxiety about how much a bottle of champagne chosen by the maitre d' of such an establishment might cost. Claudia intercepted their glance.

'Tonight is on the house,' she told them and laughed at their transparent astonishment. Over Steve's none too urgent demurral she insisted, 'No, really. It is. It's all paid for. In fact nobody pays for it. True. You have stepped into the wonderland of the advertising world. Where nobody and everybody pays.

Where it's all sleight of hand, funny money and back-slapping camaraderie. Hey!'

'How come?' Steve managed to ask.

'Its all part of the good news I mentioned to you Dad,' Lewis said. 'But you told me that you and Ma had something you wanted to talk about. Let's do that first.' He leaned forward expectantly. 'So come on, spill the beans, what are you two up to?'

'Your father and I are going walkabout,' Cathy announced. We're giving up work, for a while at least, and we're going up to the Kimberley. To swim in the Mitchell Falls and to rattle along the Gibb River Road.'

'Good on you!' Lewis all but cheered. Cathy beamed at a stunned Steve and squeezed his thigh under the table as Carter appeared with a foaming bottle of vintage Krug.

Each of them had consumed two glasses of the champagne and their entree before they finished exploring the possibilities of Steve and Cathy's upcoming nomadic lifestyle and Steve asked,

'That's enough about us. What's this news you have?'

Cathy felt her heart miss a beat. She didn't dare risk a glance at Steve.

CHAPTER TEN

'Well,' Lewis looked first at one parent and then at the other, 'you two are going bush and I'm going to China.'

'China,' they both repeated, parrot-like, and truly stunned. The news was so totally different from what they had anticipated that for a moment neither of them could manage more than saying again, 'China?'

' Yes. China. You know that big country to the north of us. Most populous country in the world. World's biggest market. Hey, you two stop looking like someone just removed your brains and ask me why.'

'Why?' Steve asked as requested.

'I've been made an offer I can't refuse,' he joked and, disappointed that neither parent followed through, he continued, 'I've been headhunted. All because of Claudia,' he put his hand on top of his wife's, which lay on the table and Cathy again thought how well they both looked.

'It happened right in this room,' he looked about at the tables filled with well-dressed, well-behaved, apparently affluent diners. The glamour enhanced by low, soft lighting.

'Claudia insisted that I accompany her to an event hosted by her company. You know how much I loathe those sort of gatherings Ma,' he turned toward her and grimaced.

She smiled at the memory of the scruffy uni student he had been, forever agitating for political and social change, expressing in vulgar language his opinions about community, religious and social leaders and ideas, wanting to make the world a better place and doing his bit by joining Greenpeace and Amnesty International; by bringing back homeless students and stray dogs and by doing pro bono work for the Aboriginal Legal Service in Redfern.

'She dragged me along, more or less kicking and screaming. I really wasn't in the mood for the sort of people who work in the advertising industry.' Steve and Cathy murmured sympathetically. Cathy noticed that Claudia smiled to herself. 'It was a big bash for their international parent company. All bells, all whistles, as only the advertising business does it. T.O.T.T.' When his parents looked puzzled by the acronym, he translated; 'Totally Over The Top. Advertising, media talk. Its infectious.' He looked sheepish.

'My plan was to enjoy the view...' they all looked out of the windows toward the Opera House, which glowed, fecund and opalescent, beside the dark, magnificent strength of the Harbour Bridge. Yin and yang, Cathy thought. '...and to avoid talking to anyone,' Lewis continued, 'because I assumed I wouldn't

CHAPTER TEN

have anything in common with them. Just get stuck into the food and the booze, both of which were totally excellent, of course. So I was pretty well half-cut by the time this American cornered me. He was about my age and I didn't know him from a bar of soap but he seemed determined to hang in there even after I'd given him a pretty hefty serve about American corporate greed, their refusal to let their troops come under the jurisdiction of the International Criminal Court and the erosion of some basic human rights in the States in all the follow-up to September 11.'

'Sounds pretty heavy,' Steve said.

Lewis chuckled. 'Well you know how I can get a bit carried away with a few under the belt, a bit simplistic and immature really.'

Cathy noted an underlying change in her son.

'Anyway the outcome of it was that two days later, a Saturday, the phone rang really early and it was this same guy. He apologised for the hour of the call, explained he had tracked down our number through one of Claudia's office colleagues and said that he would like to go for a surf. Seems that in my inebriated condition I had offered to show him what real surf is like. He wanted to go right then, because he had an afternoon flight to catch. Fifteen minutes later he turned up in a cab. Thank god Bondi was pumping.'

Their entree settings were cleared and Cathy waved her hand over her glass as the sommelier proffered the wine. The champagne was having its effect and she decided she needed a clearer head for this conversation.

'He was a really good surfer. Better than me,' Lewis admitted. 'But that was only the first of the surprises. He suggested brunch so we went to the Lamrock and of course a few of my mates were there and when I went to introduce him, I couldn't because I didn't even know his name! He didn't appear in the least put out by that and I started to realise he was a bit different from most of the Americans I've met. Not at all pushy. Genuinely interested in other people's points of view. Quite cool, you could even say cultured, sophisticated. We shook hands and I said, 'pleased to meet you, my name's Lewis Connolly,' and he said, 'likewise, my name's Harvey Goldstein."

Lewis gave a wry smile. 'Then,' he held up a forefinger, 'the pieces began to all come together. Goldstein, I said. Would that be the Goldstein of Shapiro, Marx and Goldstein? 'The son of the very same,' he assured me.'

'SMG,' Claudia interrupted, 'is the firm my company uses for all its international legal work. There's an office in Sydney, but the parent organisation is in New York.'

CHAPTER TEN

'Huge,' Lewis added. 'Mega-huge. The branch office here is very small beer in international terms, but big and influential by Sydney standards.'

'One of their clients,' Claudia mentioned the name of the CEO of the advertising company she worked for, 'is part owner of this restaurant, so that's why the event was held here and why tonight is on the house.'

'You scratch my back, I'll scratch yours, ' Steve suggested.

'That's the way it works,' Claudia shrugged. 'Its likely that less than a third of the people here are paying for their meal themselves. Either their company is, or its some form or other of payback.'

Cathy glanced around again at the full tables, the shaven-headed waiters in long white shirt-sleeves and full-length black wrap-around aprons and saw the maitre d' welcoming a table of late starters in his engaging manner. The well-oiled world of money, Cathy thought, so different from the hardscrabble of the Education Department.

'And I would like you to join the company,' he said, just like that!' Lewis laughed and repeated, 'Just like that, and I told him, sure... why not? It was so outrageous.'

They all smiled at such outrageousness

'Pretty amazing to offer a job to someone you've only just met, under less than propitious circumstances,' Steve commented.

'That seems to be Harvey's style,' Lewis grinned. 'Later on I found out that he'd had quite a search done on me. His P.A. had spent the forty-eight hours checking out my legal credentials. Various cases I'd worked on. Somehow or other he'd even seen a C.V., which I'd sent in with a job application to McAllister and McAllister a year or so ago.'

'I know a lot more about him and his modus operandi now than I did a month ago. So I know that if I don't perform, I'll be out just as quick as I came in. At that Saturday brunch he told me that he could find scores of equally smart legal brains to employ, but what particularly appealed to him was my no bullshit style,' Lewis's grin broadened. 'True. He also said that he liked the way I think outside the box. That's Americaspeak. And my zany personality. His words.'

They all laughed. Then Steve asked, 'And China? What has this to do with going to China?'

'Well,' Lewis began, 'You probably know that over the past few years there has been this big, in fact vast, change in regulations in China which has pushed up the allowable holdings by foreign companies as joint venturers in their funds management companies from 33% to 49% and there's been colossal growth in

CHAPTER TEN

the industry there. If anything, we're a little late getting in on the action but, according to Harvey the potential for growth is still enormous.'

'I didn't even know China had funds management companies, ' Cathy felt a degree of surprise bordering on shock.

'You're not the only one,' Lewis told her, 'they're coming up on the inside like gangbusters and we're too busy worrying about the Bledisloe Cup to have time to notice.'

'And that's where SMG and I come in. They are the in-house lawyers for...' he mentioned a large overseas investment bank, '...who, as you know, have branches here. Incidentally the part owner of this restaurant, who Claudia told you about... her boss, is on the board of directors of that bank,'

Cathy thought, but didn't say, that it was highly unlikely that Claudia's boss, the advertising guru, restaurateur and now revealed as a director on the board of an investment bank, ever did anything that was even remotely incidental.

'Harvey came out here in small part to represent his father, but in very large part to be the driving force behind SMG's push into China. They need lawyers to deal with the CSRC....'

'China Securities Regulatory Commission,' Claudia translated.'

'...to deal with the investment negotiations for the various parties involved.'

'Through a translator.' Steve stated.

'Of course,' Lewis agreed. 'We have a really good one from here. China born, Melbourne educated. Totally bi-lingual. And another who's Hong Kong based, attended Yale. Both very bright. They have to be. The other two people in the team are a couple of Group Security Strategic Analysts, who are highly experienced in dealing with mergers and acquisitions across the whole bank.'

'Group Security Strategic Analysts!' Steve repeated dryly. 'High power stuff, eh.'

'I know, Dad. But Americans love that sort of thing. And the bottom line is that a lot of people are going to make a motser. When Harvey Goldstein talks about China, he sounds like a crackpot religious messiah. He truly sees us as riding the big new wave. He even uses the phrase Manifest Destiny. They can't help it you know, Americans. They drink it in with their mother's milk and spend the rest of their lives regurgitating it. Burrrp! Burrp!'

Again they all laughed.

'Foreign investors can go one of two ways,' Lewis went on, 'either buy a stake in existing funds or greenfield, that is build from scratch. I have nothing to do with those decisions. What I'll be doing is talk-

CHAPTER TEN

ing with the local legal outfits and then assisting in the negotiations. I've already met with the translators and also with some other legals who have been working in the field for other firms, an Australian, an American and a Brit, to get some feel for what to expect.'

'They all tell me,' Lewis picked up his knife and laid it back on the spotless, crisp, white tablecloth at an angle of forty-five degrees, 'that if that...' he pointed at the knife, '...represents the manner of western-style negotiation, then this...' he drew imaginary loops back and forth in the air just above the knife, '...is what to expect when you negotiate in China.'

'What about bribery? Corruption?' Steve queried.

Lewis shook his head. 'A definite no-no. A bullet in the back of the neck is what you get for any attempt to rip off the system in China. Perhaps they should try that in the US,' he laughed. 'No, just joking! But seriously, Stern Hu got off lightly with ten years over that Rio Tinto business, only because he was an Australian citizen.'

'You're not going to have to move to China are you?' Cathy looked anxious.

'No, Ma, no,' he reassured her. 'But I will be spending perhaps up to two weeks of every month there, at least in the initial stages while the business gets set up. First trip will probably be the week after next.' He looked excited 'Shanghai to begin with. But there's also talk of Taipei.' He paused before adding. 'The money's pretty solid too.'

'It's a long way from Greenpeace and Redfern,' Steve commented.

Lewis nodded. Claudia remarked quietly, 'about time.'

Cathy thought, she's helping him mature, and said 'Congratulations darling. We're very proud of you.' Her son leant across and gave her a kiss on the cheek. 'Thanks Ma.'

Their main courses had all been served so graciously during this conversation that it was only now Cathy realised her barramundi lay before her. There was a pause in conversation while everyone began to eat and then Steve asked, referring to the legal firm where Lewis had been employed for the past eight years, 'Do O'Grady and Douglas know about this?'

'Oh yes, and they're cool. They knew that I've been looking around.' Lewis assured him. 'They have been great to me over the years. Giving me time away to go shooting off for Amnesty and to Greenpeace demos. But I've been feeling for a while that I've outgrown them and Harvey Goldstein just came along at the right moment. Its going to be a steep learning

CHAPTER TEN

curve.' He was obviously happy about this. 'But I feel I'm ready for that. I've been sort of coasting along. This is a big challenge. I feel as though my life is changing and I feel good about it. I've reached a watershed, made some big decisions.'

'Decisions like Ruby and the baby,' Steve suggested.

Eleven

'Ruby and the baby,' Lewis repeated and looked toward Claudia. It was their turn to be extremely surprised.

There appeared to be a sudden general lull in the conversation in the restaurant, as if all the diners were waiting for Lewis to continue.

Cathy and Steve remained silent. Cathy could feel the pulse flickering in her eyelid.

'I had been planning to tell you both,' Lewis said. 'To talk to you about it.'

Cathy and Steve still did not speak. Cathy couldn't trust herself to do so. She could feel hot tears fill her eyes.

'I've just been so busy. It needed to be when we had quiet uninterrupted time and that's so hard to find what with all of us working flat out, and Sam and everything...' his voice trailed away.

'Your mother and I...,' Steve began and Cathy realised from the shaky timbre of his voice how hard all this was for him. She felt a surge of love toward him. '...understand this is something you and Claudia,' he made an inclusive gesture, 'have decided to do and that you probably didn't think it was necessary to consider that we might feel...'

'That's not true Dad.' Lewis interrupted but Steve continued, '...a degree of responsibility for what will after all be our grandchild.' He held up his hand, as again Lewis went to interrupt. 'Its important to explain what being grandparents means to us.' He turned to Cathy. She took a deep breath and attempted to smile at her son and daughter-in-law. Her voice was trembling too.

'Well,' she began, 'you must both know how much we love Sam.'

'Of course we do Ma.'

Claudia nodded.

Cathy continued. 'I hadn't anticipated feeling like I do about being a grandmother. To feel such a gut-wrenchingly visceral, yet pure, love. Pure because I expect and demand nothing in return. It has none of the hideously complex emotional ties I felt embroiled in with you and Sophie. He's a clean sheet, a new start. He's his own man but as well as that, he's our

CHAPTER ELEVEN

future.' She looked around the table. 'All of us. He's our shot at immortality.'

'Because I've been through it from start to finish with you,' she looked toward Lewis, 'and Sophie, I have a real knowledge of how quickly it all happens. Baby. Toddler. School and gone. In a flash. So with Sam I am careful to treasure him. He's a little piece of magic that has dropped into our lives. A transitory gift.'

'Also, by now,' she gave a self-deprecating smile, ' I am hopefully not so driven by my own ego. Its as if there's less capital M me in my head and in its place there's more room for Sam and his fantastic fresh take on life. He challenges the habits and thought patterns I have fallen into and makes me feel I have been walking around with my eyes wide shut.'

Steve nodded in agreement.

'And the other really good thing is that there is no challenge between us. Sam doesn't need to establish himself in defiance; he doesn't need to get out from under our shadow. Because of that he can in some ways be more relaxed with us. So I like to think its an important relationship for Sam too'

'Its also very sobering,' she tried a big smile, 'to realise that whatever memories he has of us, in his mind we will always be old.'

They were all silent for a while then Lewis said, 'All of this can apply to Ruby's baby too Ma.'

Cathy nodded. 'I think I am beginning to understand that this could be true.'

A cigar chomping obese diner left his table, brandy glass in hand, and waddled his ungainly way to an adjoining group where a chair was brought so he could sit with them. Everyone seemed to know everyone else.

It was Claudia who spoke.

'I'm truly sorry that we haven't made time to talk all this through with you both. I can understand something of how you feel, because you've been such good grandparents to Sam. We don't get around to telling you this and how much we appreciate everything you do for him and us.' She gave a little sigh. 'It's one of the worst things about a rushed life. Not making time to say and do the things you should, until sometimes it's too late. There really has been a lot happening in our lives. '

The two women gave each other a smile of understanding and acceptance.

Then Claudia looked inquiringly at Lewis.

'Not yet,' he responded. 'Let's talk about Ruby and her baby first.'

CHAPTER ELEVEN

Steve spoke. 'So, is it okay to ask why you've decided to father this woman's baby?'

'Of course it is Dad. But to begin with you have to call her Ruby, not 'this woman'. In fact you've met her.'

Steve looked surprised.

'A couple of years ago when her Nan, Daisy Jacobs, who sees Mum at Wylies in the morning...'

'It was Daisy who told Cathy about...' Steve paused, '...Ruby...and the baby.'

'That'd be right. Daisy has probably told half of Sydney. You'd think she was having the baby. And in a way she is. Like you two with Sam, she sees this as her one chance for going on. But with perhaps more reason. More of that in a minute. Lets go back a bit. You met Ruby the day you picked Sophie up from the Mater because her clapped out car had boiled over and more or less blown up while she was driving to work.

Steve nodded and smiled at the memory of his daughter who had eased her car into the side of the road and then fled in panic at how much it was going to cost to be towed out of the way of the morning rush-hour traffic. She'd taken a cab the short remaining distance to work and phoned him from there to ask for help. Quite by chance he had been not that far away, on his way to a meeting with a client and had driven via the hospital hydrotherapy pool to pick up

Sophie. They were joined by a young woman, who seemed to know his daughter and who offered to come back with them, to help.   They'd driven to the deserted car, which, by the time they reached it, was about to be booked for illegal parking.

Steve remembered how Sophie and the other woman had engaged in light-hearted sexual banter with two tow-truck operators who arrived fortuitously at the scene and hooked the battered old Morris Minor convertible to their truck. Steve felt slightly flustered that what he remembered best about the occasion was the woman's figure hugging short shorts.

' Slim,' he waved his hands, 'dark-haired and ah...quite tall.'

'That's right Dad,' Lewis grinned. 'I thought you'd remember! Good legs!'

The truck had towed the car to a repair station and with an inoffensive display of macho charm; the drivers had told the two attractive women that they'd halve the towing charge. Steve had then driven the two of them back to the hospital so that Sophie could start work and her friend could rescue the patient she had left exercising with the physio in the rehab pool. At the time it was not apparent that this friend was Daisy's granddaughter and what Steve also recalled was feeling his age as he listened to their giggling banter while they relived their adventure. So, that was

CHAPTER ELEVEN

Ruby. He had a memory of glancing at her in his rear vision mirror and of thinking what an attractive, wide mouth and generous smile she had.

'Not what you expected,' Lewis delighted in his father's discomfiture.

'She's an unusual girl,' Claudia agreed. We met her that same day, in the evening. She and Sophie were having a swim in the Bay. They'd become instant friends and we also got along with her straight away. Ruby stayed with Daisy for a while to help ease her into her new hip. It was a pretty massive op. We saw a lot of her, got to know each other pretty well and after she moved back to her own place at Bondi Junction we kept up the contact and the friendship developed.'

The fat man continued to chew wetly on his un-lit cigar. It seemed that even he dared not light up in such surroundings. The other dinner guests at his table resembled supplicants, leaning forward, hanging on his every loud word, which mostly seemed to be about either himself or shares and stock options.

Steve said, 'She is attractive and I take your word for it that she's unusual. But still, it's a leap from that to all that's involved in fathering her child. A child who will be raised by...'

'...a couple of lesbians,' Lewis completed his sentence.

'The bottom line,' Claudia spoke, 'is that Ruby will be a great mother. I'm sure of that. She wants so badly to have a child of her own. This is not just some passing whim. She and Kit have lived together for four years. They're a solid couple. They're buying their own place. Ruby's a specialist nurse working in palliative care. A tough job, not taken on by many younger women and Kit's a senior ambulance driver. Another hard call. They're neither of them lightweights playing at Mums and Dads. They've both been around a bit. They're reaching their mid- thirties and they know they're running out of time.'

Steve looked pained. 'I have to say this. Because we need to be honest. It just doesn't feel...'

'...natural.' Again Lewis filled in for his father, who nodded. 'Because it isn't,' his son concluded, 'for us.'

'I'm uncomfortable with imagining what they do.' Steve's voice was strained. He looked down at the table and fiddled with his remaining cutlery.

They waited for Steve to regain his composure. Then Lewis said, 'I grew up in a household where we all lay around on the deck, or walked from bathroom to bedroom, with no clothes on. I don't think you've ever had a nightdress have you Ma?'

CHAPTER ELEVEN

Cathy smiled and shook her head as Lewis went on, 'so I don't have any trouble with imagining you two jumping each other's bones. But people who haven't seen their parents naked, and perhaps that's most people, would be uncomfortable imagining what they do. So its mostly all a matter of experience and,' he added, 'keeping an open mind.'

'Have either of them ever had boyfriends?' Cathy asked.

'Not Kit,' Claudia told them. 'She has said that she knew she was gay from her earliest memories. When she was a child. Long before she was a teenager. But for Ruby it's a different story. Its been a hard path.'

She waited, perhaps for Lewis to speak, but when he didn't she continued. 'Ruby's Mum, Esther, was born on a ship which was on its way to Australia in 1947 with a cargo of refugees from Europe. Daisy, that's not her real name of course, its the one she took when she arrived here to help her blend in, she and her husband had been living in various DP camps. I think they were Russians, but had finished the war somehow or other in either Austria or Germany. Daisy has told me all this but she gets very emotional and confused. Imagine arriving here with a newborn baby, no job, no place to go and not speaking any English. I don't think Australia was exactly welcoming either.'

AN IMMACULATE CONCEPTION

'Her husband was studying industrial chemistry before the war, but with no English there was no hope of his continuing to study. Through some contacts he managed to get a job behind the scenes in a pharmacy in Bondi Junction. Daisy started work at the Bisley shirt factory, as a seamstress. She stayed there for thirty-three years. They both of them had lost all their family members so they were utterly alone. They put Esther into day-care and just worked non-stop. Daisy also took in washing and ironing and did weekend cleaning jobs as well. Her husband had a second job as a janitor. He never really felt at home here. He never spoke anything but Yiddish at home.'

Cathy, Steve and Lewis remained silent, listening to Claudia.

'Esther was fifteen when her father committed suicide.'

'Oh god,' Cathy sighed and closed her eyes as if that would shut out the horror.

'She came back from school and found him hanging from the kitchen door. He'd left a note saying that he loved them but he couldn't go on living in the black void, asking them to forgive him and detailing all the family finances. It seems he had waited until the flat they had purchased was paid off. Daisy told me he never really recovered from what he experienced during the war and from the extinction of his

CHAPTER ELEVEN

entire family. Who are we to judge when we can't possibly even begin to imagine.'

Claudia stopped speaking and after a while Lewis began, 'Esther never went back to school. She started work at the same shirt factory as her mother. I get the feeling she just shut down emotionally and perhaps she didn't feel safe anywhere except around her Mum. She didn't go out or have any boyfriends or anything like that. Then, when she was in her early twenties, out of the blue, a relative, albeit a distant one, turned up. He was about the same age as Esther and claimed to be a cousin, or an uncle twice removed, something like that. But whether he was or he wasn't, or whoever he really was, he seemed to know their family history and perhaps in their vulnerable condition, Daisy and Esther just wanted to believe he was family, so they both threw themselves on him; Esther more literally than her mum. She became pregnant and Carter was born.'

'Carter!' Cathy and Steve repeated in duo.

Lewis nodded.

'The maitre d'?' Cathy asked.

He nodded again.

'Is ...Ruby's...brother?'

Another nod from Lewis. 'Claudia put his name...of course Carter is only his professional name... forward for the job here when the restaurant opened. A bit of insider trading. He's a natural for it as you can see and gay also, as you no doubt realise. But it doesn't end there. Esther gave up work and stayed home to nurse Carter and next thing you know she's pregnant again, this time it's a girl, Ruby. Then this guy shoots through. Never seen or heard from him again.'

This time it was Steve. 'My god.'

'All this time Daisy kept on working,' Claudia told them, 'and between them the two women raised Carter and Ruby. Both of them have told us funny, horror stories about some of the men their mother got involved with over the years. She even married one of them briefly. But they've never had a really substantial father figure. I get the feeling that in many ways the roles have been somewhat reversed and Ruby has been the mother rather than the daughter. It's only in the last ten years or so that Esther has found some degree of peace. She lives up in the Blue Mountains in a mud brick place she's building herself. She's become a trained counsellor and works with women's groups. She's a good woman. Damaged by life, but good.'

'As for Ruby,' Lewis said, 'she has had boyfriends. But...'

Claudia added, 'we get the feeling that she is frightened of repeating her mother's mistakes. So she feels more comfortable with another woman. Carter

CHAPTER ELEVEN

has always been gay. Like Kit, he says he knew he was since he was a child. So...'

'...you can see why Daisy is so happy for Ruby to be trying to become pregnant.' Lewis spread his hands, palms up, for emphasis. 'She is her only chance for what you call a shot at immortality. For a clean start. Everyone else has been wiped out. Ruby is her only way into the future.'

'Lewis and I have talked it through endlessly and come to the conclusion that this is just one small way of doing our bit,' Claudia continued.

The four of them sat back to take a breather from the conversation in their high-backed chairs. Their dinner plates had been cleared. Steve and Lewis ordered desserts. 'With extra spoons so the ladies can have a taste,' Lewis asked of the server.

The performance in the Opera House must have come to an end because a stream of people began to cascade down the full width of the steps and advance toward them across the concourse. From the change of the sound levels downstairs, Cathy judged that a number of them must have stopped in for a drink or a late evening snack.

'Are you planning on having your name on the birth certificate?' Cathy asked her son.

'That's something we're still discussing,' Lewis responded and when Steve looked puzzled Cathy explained, 'If the father is stated as 'Unknown', then Lewis would have no legal rights. All rights would be held by the birth mother, not even her same sex partner would have any rights.'

'We know its important to get this clearly sorted out,' Claudia told them, 'and we have been talking with Ruby and Kit about what we all would like, both for the child and for ourselves. Its hard, but we're trying to cover all bases.'

'Claudia and I would like my name on the birth certificate,' Lewis told them. 'We think that's best for the child. We want Ruby and Kit to regard us, and Sam, as part of their extended family. We aren't planning on financial involvement. That would be treading on their territory. In all major areas, the child would be their responsibility. But you know we're still only talking in theory. This child has yet to be conceived and they've chosen the most difficult method.'

'Home insemination.' Cathy stated.

Lewis and Claudia nodded in unison.

'You know there's only a fifteen percent chance of success within each period of fertility?' Cathy asked.

CHAPTER ELEVEN

'Yes,' Lewis responded. 'And I can tell you its not all fun.' He grimaced and the other three smiled rather awkwardly. 'We've had one dry run, so to speak, but producing sperm to order,' he shook his head, 'not good.'

'I understand,' Claudia said, 'why they prefer to try at home rather than in a clinic. It's more friendly and feels less like a medical procedure. So we'll just see how we go.'

'Coming and going from China will add complications to the timing,' Lewis added. 'So the four of us have decided to start the clinic procedure at the same time because its takes six months from when I donated the sperm to when it becomes available for insemination, what with all the medical checks they do for AIDS and HepC.'

'You've done that already?' Cathy asked, suddenly suspicious.

'Yes. We all went along to New Concepts... that's a fertility clinic ...' Cathy held back a gasp of surprise, '...and had a counselling session and then I produced a little plastic tub full of life for them.' He and Claudia smiled. Cathy remembering Sandra's cryptic remark, 'We're all in this together,' felt the pieces of the puzzle drop together.

'The doctor who runs the clinic is a good woman,' Lewis told them.

'Yes,' Cathy said quietly, 'I know that because I go to see her too! Not,' she smiled, 'because I'm trying to have another baby! I have quite enough to cope with right now thank you! ' They all laughed. 'But because Sandra's an excellent gynaecologist. I was lucky she was prepared to take me on. And, as it turns out, she's very discreet too. She didn't mention to me that you'd all been to see her. I guess for professional reasons she couldn't. This really is all in the family stuff! '

Lewis nodded in agreement. 'Nor did she mention to us that you're a client of hers, but its a comment on the fact that there are only a couple of clinics in Sydney which take on same sex couples. So it's not at all that surprising that we end up in the same one. It's hard for lesbians to become mothers. They can't adopt. They get treated like social pariahs and outcasts by everyone. The church won't even give them Communion. The government drivels on about motherhood, but there's zero political support for same sex mothers.'

'When the media get on to it, it's as if there's an unholy wave of dykes about to steal our women. Yet each year between two and three hundred women in same sex relationships have a baby. That's all. It's miniscule. Our birth rate is falling below what's

CHAPTER ELEVEN

needed just to replicate ourselves so unless we have a massive immigration programme we're doomed just to coast down to a slow extinction.'

'End of rave.' Claudia held up her hand and they all laughed.

The desserts arrived. Creamy affairs decorated with green sticks of angelica and elegant chocolate swirls.

Before he spoiled this perfection Steve, who had been looking uncomfortable, asked, 'Your donation, to the clinic, will it be...'

'...generally available? Lewis prompted.

Steve nodded.

'No. It was given under very specific terms, one of which was that it was only to be used to enable Ruby to conceive. You needn't worry Dad. You're not going to have scores of unknown grandchildren running around out there.'

Steve looked somewhat relieved. 'Its just that...'

'...it's okay Dad. Men and women have different approaches to all this and your worries are exactly the ones I had.'

The two men exchanged a conspiratorial glance and attacked their deserts.

Cathy watched as the fat man, cigar in pudgy hand, and his entourage, made an extended and showy exit from the restaurant accompanied all the way by Carter who, Cathy was happy to note, managed the difficult trick of being polite and friendly without appearing fawning. Having farewelled them, Carter came across to their table, one of the last to still have diners seated and after Lewis had invited him, drew up a chair.

'I hope you all enjoyed your meals,' he seemed genuinely concerned. They all assured him that it had been a splendid meal and he looked pleased. He offered them a brandy but they all demurred on the grounds of driving home and having early starts.

'Then I would like you to try my really excellent decaff,' he offered and when that was ordered from the ever attentive but never intrusive server, Cathy asked, 'This may be an insensitive question but do you have some regulation for your staff that insists on them all shaving their heads?'

Carter laughed with genuine amusement and Cathy noticed his wide warm smile and thought that in this he must resemble his sister.

'No,' he assured her. 'It just happens to be the look of the moment.

The coffee and petit fours were served and Carter leant toward Cathy and Steve.

'I won't interrupt your family dinner any longer. I just wanted to say a huge thank you from my

CHAPTER ELEVEN

family. Your son has a big heart and is doing a wonderful thing. He is giving life and hope and a future to people who have been crushed by experience and nature and who were about to slip away into oblivion.'

Cathy felt her eyes fill with tears once more.
'To Claudia too, of course, a big thank you. But I want you to know that whatever the outcome is of these decisions, you can be truly proud of your son and of yourselves as his mother and father. He is who he is because he has you two as his parents.'

He stood up, gave his sister's smile. 'Enjoy your coffee and I look forward to seeing you at the handfasting,' and was gone.

No one spoke for some long time, each busy with their own thoughts and emotions, then it was the practical Steve again who asked, 'Handfasting?'

And Claudia who explained to him, 'Ruby and Kit are getting married. Except that of course they can't get married in a legal sense. But they are going through a ceremony, which is called a handfasting. It's a centuries old English word that means to pledge, to betroth, to join solemnly by the hand. They want to make a public demonstration of their love in front of family and friends.'

'They asked me,' Lewis said, 'if I thought that you would like to come and I said...'

'Yes. Of course. We'd love to come.' Cathy spoke up.

'Good,' Claudia opened a beaded evening bag and handed across an envelope. 'I brought the invitation. Its on not this Saturday but the Saturday following.'

'Oh damn!' Cathy frowned. 'That's the weekend Mum's coming up. She wants to have a family lunch with everyone. It's important because she's...'

'She can come to the handfasting too,' Lewis interrupted quickly, 'and then we can have a family get together on the Sunday. It'd be great. I'd like her to meet Ruby.'

'Its a lot to ask of an eighty-four year old woman,' Cathy responded, 'Especially as she's dying.'

Lewis and Claudia looked very shocked.

'Dying?!' Lewis's voice was brittle with emotion. 'What d'you mean? How come? I didn't even know Nana had been ill? Why didn't you tell me?'

'I don't think she's actually ill,' Cathy told them. 'And she hasn't even told us she feels she's close to dying. But she asked us to make a sudden visit to Canberra. We just came back this morning. While we were there she gave me my father's cap and medals and the flag that draped his coffin. She also asked me to arrange a family luncheon in Sydney, as soon as possible, with everyone there. That's something she

CHAPTER ELEVEN

has never asked for before. In addition we found out, by chance, that last week she arranged and paid for her own funeral.'

It was Claudia who broke their silence by commenting in a quiet voice; 'That takes courage.'

'Good on you Nana,' Lewis murmured.

'She's almost eighty-five,' Claudia spoke to her husband in a gentle tone, 'and that's a good innings.'

He nodded slowly. 'I guess so,' he paused, 'but I'll miss her. We haven't seen enough of her in the last couple of years. Too busy. Always too busy. 'He chastised himself. 'But I just like knowing she's there. If you know what I mean.'

They were all quiet once more, then Lewis said, 'In a way, perhaps, it wouldn't be so bad to sense when your time is coming to an end. I don't think I'd like to know exactly, but it would be good to know in advance that I had eighty-four or so years to make something of my life. Its the not knowing when and how that's so hard.'

Cathy had a sudden image of Dr. Forbes' gloved hands holding the biopsy of her cervix.

'But if she is dying,' Lewis forced his voice to lighten in an attempt to lift the sombre mood, 'then its all the more important that she meets Ruby. And also that she hears our other major piece of news.'

'China?' Steve said.

AN IMMACULATE CONCEPTION

'No,' Claudia looked triumphant. 'Its what we came here to tell you tonight. I'm pregnant!'

The few remaining diners turned to stare with disapproval as Cathy and Steve erupted into loud cheers.

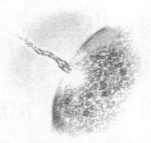

Twelve

'Well, death to birth in what you could call an emotionally full twenty-four hours,' Steve gave a huge stretch and relaxed his body under the doona. Cathy slipped in beside him. 'Yes. And its not over yet.'

After the announcement of the impending new baby the four of them had stayed another half hour in the restaurant, by which time they were the last patrons and even the lights on the Opera House had been switched off. They also decided that another bottle of champagne was called for.

'An Australian one this time,' Carter suggested. 'Hardy's Aras. One of the best Australian sparkling wines.'

'We've been hanging out to tell you,' Lewis said as they sipped from fresh long stemmed cut glasses, 'but we wanted to wait until we were sure. It's still very early days. Around seven or eight weeks.'

'I thought you looked particularly well,' Cathy told her daughter-in-law.

'I feel pretty good,' Claudia confirmed. 'A bit yukky in the mornings but otherwise okay.' She looked a little embarrassed before adding, 'I've done the Draino test and we think it's a girl.'

'The Draino test?' Steve queried.

'It's an old wives tale...' she began.

'...highly politically incorrect but,' Lewis raised both eyebrows in a mannerism which reminded Cathy of Sam, 'all that seems to become acceptable when chicks get pregnant!'

'...but they say that if, when you pour some Draino into your pee,' Claudia continued, 'it goes golden brown then its a girl. If it goes dark brown its a boy.'

They all laughed and sipped more champagne.

'I did it when I was pregnant with Sam and it went dark brown. So.'

Cathy raised her glass. 'I say here's to whatever it is. May it be healthy and happy. Have you told Sam yet?

'No, It's too soon. We'll wait until I start to show.'

CHAPTER TWELVE

Cathy experienced a moment of anxiety and sadness for Sam, for his loss of place as the sole centre of their emotional universe.

Lewis seemed to sense this. 'He'll be right. By the time the baby comes he'll be almost going to school so he'll have plenty to occupy him. It had to happen some time. We've kept putting it off for one reason or another. It somehow seemed a much bigger commitment than having just one child. Then this China job offered a bit more financial security.'

'It was deciding to help Ruby,' Claudia added, 'that was the clincher for us. It was so complicated and difficult a decision for her and Kit that it made our indecision appear incredibly selfish, our ease of choice such an unearned luxury.

'So Ma now instead of just one grandchild to dote on, you'll have three to enjoy watching grow up.'

Cathy had another flash of Dr. Forbes gloved hands.

'I certainly hope so,' she said.

On their drive home through the quiet lamp lit streets of the Eastern Suburbs Steve commented on Cathy's seemingly sudden expertise on the subjects of home insemination, IVF and the various legal ramifications of birth certificate details.

'You wouldn't have been spending time on the dreaded Web would you?' he teased her.

'No. I've been chatting with Sandra Forbes.' To fend off more questions she talked for the rest of the short journey including some remarks about how both Lewis and Claudia appeared to be happier, more settled and to have matured.

'Another demonstration of punctuated equilibrium perhaps,' Steve quipped as he drove into their garage.

Steve rolled towards her in the bed and she rested her head in the basin of his shoulder.

'You mean there's more to look forward to? He buried his chin in the thick dark hair on the top of her head and rubbed it back and forth in an anticipatory way.

She turned her face up to his. Her expression was fearful. She spoke in short staccato sentences. 'I'm afraid so. It could be that I have cancer of the cervix. That's why I've been with Sandra Forbes. She asked me to come and see her. That's where I was this afternoon. With my phone switched off. That's why I needed to swim.'

He gripped her and held her tight with both arms.

CHAPTER TWELVE

In the deep silence a dog barked. Twice. Far off. They heard Digger respond, half-heartedly, in a sleepy voice, from his basket in the downstairs rumpus room.

She then repeated to him the medical information that Sandra had given her and imperceptibly she began to cry. Tears of grief and loss and fear. 'It's a bugger. I don't want to die. Not yet. I feel as though I am only just beginning to live, to have some inkling of why we're here, what its all about. I have so much left to do.'

Steve gently licked the teardrops from her closed eyelids and cheeks. She remembered how touched she had been when he had done that to both Sophie and Lewis when they were small children. The memory made her cry all the more. His arms cradled and rocked her.

'So that was the reason for tonight's out of the blue announcement of our impending trip to the Kimberley.

She nodded, half smothered in his arms.

'Well that's where we're going,' his voice expressed determination. 'Soon. This news is just a wake-up call to start us on our way. You're going to get this fixed up. We are, together. Nothing's surer.'

He loosened his grip so he could hold her at a little distance and look into her eyes. 'Believe me,' he said with resonance and she felt she could.

In the morning she found she had inexplicably slept through her internal alarm clock and woke to find it already full daylight with Steve gone from beside her.

Stumbling, half-asleep, out through the house to his office in what had been an old shed at the far end of the garden, she found him already seated at the computer.

'Good morning,' he beamed at her with happy smile. 'I've been looking up cervical cancer and all info and prognoses look good! See I told you; the Web is a marvellous tool. Speaking of which, I want you to go back to bed and I will bring you in a cup of tea and myself.'

When she looked doubtful about the wisdom of this he insisted.

'Happiness is the great cure-all. And afterwards we can look through all this together.' The printer began to whir and churn out paper.

In mid-morning they swam across Coogee Bay and back together. The weather was sparkling and the sky cloudless, but because it was a winter weekday

CHAPTER TWELVE

they were the only people in that part of the ocean. On her way out, Cathy swam over a tiny school of small colourless rays, perhaps half a dozen of the creatures. She wondered if they were a family.

Snuggled into their cosy fibre-pile jackets, because for a while after a swim in cold water their body temperatures continued to fall, they crossed the road from the beach to the plastic walled enclosure of a small café where they sat under the outdoor gas heaters, looking out at the passing traffic and the beach.

They were hardly seated when the owner, a slim Chinese man probably in his late thirties, came to take their simple brunch order. In the two years since he had bought the business and had it open for up to fifteen hours a day, he had so improved the look and atmosphere of what was essentially an unpretentious cheap eats café, that the place was now as packed at weekends as the beachside cafes in Bronte, despite the menu being rather less trendy. In the sincerest form of flattery, two more cafés of similar style had opened up to one side. And from the hectic building works presently underway, it seemed there was another one about to be opened on the other side.

'G'day Mr. Connolly,' the proprietor struggled with the double l's, 'you taking day off?'

'Indeed Cheng Guan, and we're intending to take quite a few more.'

'Good on you,' he pronounced the three words separately. 'You work hard long enough time.'

They gave their meal orders.

'I am sorry about big mess and noise next door,' Cheng Guan's beam of satisfaction contradicted his apology.

'More competition,' Steve sounded consoling.

'No. No. This one my place too.'

They congratulated him on his expanding business.

'Yes. Very good this one.' He nodded. 'For my son. When he is older.'

Cathy and Steve had sometimes seen the son referred to. He was in his early teens and sat with his younger sister at a small table at the far end of the takeaway counter inside the cafe. There, in the light summer evenings they did their homework for school and extra tuition classes, while their mother and other relatives cooked, served and cleaned up.

'Cheng Guan and Sons,' the owner beamed with anticipation of empire.

'Our son is having another baby,' Steve said with competitive pride. Cheng Guan had met Sam many times.

'Oh very good, very good.' He seemed genuinely pleased.

CHAPTER TWELVE

'He's actually having two.' Cathy told him, carried away by the proliferation of joy.

'Two babies. Twins.' Cheng Guan pronounced the word as if he had just learnt it.

'No.' Steve told him. 'Two babies, two different wives...women,' he stumbled in his explanation.

'Oh, very, very good,' a completely unfazed Cheng Guan concluded, 'Australia need much more babies,' and hurried off to get their meals underway.

Cathy and Steve laughed together.

'No hang-ups there! Steve said.

'Just as long as its sons,' Cathy shook her head.

'Should we tell him about the Draino test?'

'They don't need it. I read the figures somewhere about the number of new ultra-sound machines being set up in China. It was something ludicrous like two hundred a week. Mostly so they can find out if a foetus is male or female. With dire consequences for the females.'

The fried eggs on toast with a side order of grilled tomatoes were served within five minutes.

Warmed by a large mug of hot chocolate Steve asked, 'are you still sure you're up to going in to your office this afternoon?'

Cathy nodded. 'Definitely. I want to clear the air.'

AN IMMACULATE CONCEPTION

'I want to clear the air,' Cathy told her Director of Department. Claude Borsellino leant his head on his intertwined fingers and studied her over the top of his rimless half-glasses. She had been pleasantly surprised when he had responded to her telephoned request for an urgent meeting by telling her that he had a free half hour that afternoon. He waited for her to continue.

'I've decided not to pursue my application for the position of Assistant Director.'

Claude Borsellino pursed his lips, gave a small sigh, but said nothing.

'For personal and family reasons.'

He still remained silent and looking at him Cathy thought he appeared sad, even somewhat crushed and realised how little she knew about the personal life of this man who had devoted his entire career to this department.

She spoke again. 'Unfortunately I may need to take some time off on sick leave and I think it best if I extend that into my accrued long service leave.' She paused before adding. 'Perhaps for the full six months.'

Claude Borsellino nodded.

'The position has become available at the wrong time for me. It's all in the timing. In some ways I'm sorry.'

CHAPTER TWELVE

'And in some ways you're not,' the Director suggested. In a kind voice he added, 'I understand the conflicting emotions.'

Unexpectedly he stood up and turned away toward the big window, which gave views over North Sydney toward the City. Unsure whether this was a dismissal, Cathy was beginning to rise when he turned and said; 'I am going to tell you something that cannot go outside this room.' She settled back in her chair. 'They are going to bring in an outsider to do the job.' He sat back down, heavily. 'Some smart numbers man with degrees in business administration and economics. Knows nothing about education and cares even less. Of course this is off the record. Nothing has been said officially. It can't be, the proper procedures have to be gone through. The interview process. The pretence. Keeping people's hopes up. But it's a sham show. The political decision has been made. And its also been made clear to me that I can stay on, but they would be happier if I didn't.'

The creases in his face deepened. 'Do I stay and fight with this glorified accountant for what I have always believed matters in education or do I take the money and run. For personal and family reasons.'

Stung by the implied suspicion that she was taking the easy way out Cathy told him somewhat brusquely, 'It seems highly likely that I have cervical cancer and will require an operation.'

'That's bad luck,' Claude Borsellino realised she had taken offence and added kindly. 'I'm really sorry. I didn't for one moment not believe you. Your honesty has always been apparent. Its just that I loathe those anodyne catch-all phrases.'

Cathy softened her facial expression. 'Nothing is for certain yet, I'm having extra tests done and even if it does turn out to be cancer, the gynaecologist is quite optimistic about the outcome. But all this has coincided with my husband deciding that he wants to go bush, so it seems an opportune time to combine my health demands with his very real need for a change of pace.'

'You'll miss your grandson,' he smiled. He had often commented on the growing portrait file of Sam on her desk.

'Yes. I will. But I have something to look forward to when we get back. We have another one on the way.'

'Congratulations...'

'...Oops!' She pulled a little face of alarm.' That's off the record too. They haven't told anyone else yet.'

'Say no more,' Claude Borsellino nodded, smiled and then a spasm of pain crossed his face.

CHAPTER TWELVE

'We've just lost our grandchildren...' Cathy gave a little cry of alarm. 'My son and his wife have separated and she has taken their three children to her family in Italy.'

Cathy felt a chill sense of immediate empathy. 'I am so sorry.'

He suddenly looked very old. 'My wife...' he gave a deep sigh, '...she is distraught. She is a very Italian mama so she loves her son,' he raised his hands in a gesture of despair, 'but she knows it was his playing up which caused the problems. So she is torn, very torn. She loves her bad son and she adores her grandchildren. She is talking about going back to Italy. Going back she calls it. Like it will be the same as when she left Sicily almost half a century ago as a little girl. I daren't tell her about the changes in the department. If I did she would say, throw it all in and come back with me. But I don't feel Italian. I like to visit of course. But Australia is my home. I've been here fifty years too. When I speak dialect in my father's village they fall about laughing. I sound to them like Percy Wooster would to you.'

He made another despairing gesture. 'All this uproar because my son can't keep his pants on.'

In an atmosphere of shared confidences, Cathy told Claude Borsellino about Lewis's decision to father Ruby's baby.

'Children!' he said with a touch of venom in his voice. 'They can always manage to chuck one in from left field just when you are least expecting it.' He thought a little more before adding, 'I don't think my wife would approve because the church is against it of course. But if she had to choose between having three grandchildren living in Italy and three living in Australia, even if one of them was being raised by a lesbian couple, there would be no contest!'

On her way through from the Director of Department's office to her own, Cathy forced herself to greet everyone in her usual cheerful manner. Responses were awkward and muted. The knowledge she now had of the State political machinations at work made her feel sad and a trifle guilty. She caught only a brief glimpse of Jane Howard's head as she rounded a workstation to one side and disappeared.

In the quiet of her own office Cathy began the massive task of reallocating her workload by beginning to make lists of suggestions as to who could take up the immediate slack caused by her sudden departure and where information about her tasks could be spread so as to minimise the impact on her colleagues. It was a strategy, which she and Claude Borsellino had worked out together in the hope of minimising disruption.

CHAPTER TWELVE

'Pat has a good handle on most of this,' Cathy had told him.

'Oh yes, I realise.' He had given a knowing smile. 'The figures she put in for you on Friday, even the signature, was ample evidence of that.'

'Mmm,' Cathy had nodded but not looked up from the notes she was making.

Cathy was glad that Pat was off on a flexiday, taking her son for another of his innumerable visits to hospital. It would be easier to talk matters through with her over a drink on the weekend.

The weekend. That reminded her. She rang Sophie's mobile. An abrupt message told her to leave her number. She rang her home number and was accosted by the same demand. She wondered why it was considered cool to be so abrupt.

'Hello darling. It's your ma. Hope your day went well. Just to let you know that Nana is coming up the weekend after next and has asked me to organise a family luncheon on the Sunday.' She mentioned the date. 'At our place. She is very much looking forward to seeing you, so I do hope you don't have any other unbreakable arrangements. Would you call me back as soon as you can to confirm that? Thank you darling.' She paused. 'And by the way the message on your phones is...' Click. The recording machine stopped.

Tom's mobile number was either unavailable or switched off and when she phoned his home number she wished that had been too because it was answered by Deidre who coldly informed her; 'I have no idea where my husband is and I am not taking messages for him.'

'Deidre this is Cathy,' she informed her in case for some strange reason her sister-in-law hadn't recognised her voice.

'I realise that and my answer is still the same.'

Cathy thought she detected a catch in her voice as she suggested, 'you could try leaving a message with his personal assistant at his office. I haven't seen or heard from him since Friday evening. He came by and collected some things and then took off with his latest girlfriend. I gave him an ultimatum. Its either her, or me and the girls.'

'Oh Deidre how...'

Deidre cut across her. 'This is his last chance. I won't be bought off again with holidays in Italy and diamond rings. I told him that I will not continue to be humiliated. If he contacts you, that's the message you can give him from me.'

Cathy sensed that she was about to hang up and quickly said, 'Deidre I'm really sorry about all this, but I was calling because my mother, Elizabeth, is coming up to Sydney and wanted to see the whole

CHAPTER TWELVE

family together, she's not at all well and ...' she could feel herself babbling foolishly. As if a woman who had just had such a conversation with her husband would be attracted by the idea of a family get-together.

'Ah, his mother...' There was distaste in her tone, '...wants to see him. Now, to choose between his girlfriend and his ailing mother... that would be a tough call for Tom. Goodbye.'

Thirteen

The party was well underway by the time Cathy and Steve arrived at the Edwards' farewell. The front security door was unlocked and tracking the sounds of loud conversation and decidedly uninhibited laughter they walked along the hall past the downstairs bedrooms and bathroom, down a few steps into the empty sitting room and through to the large kitchen crammed with guests.

Beyond the throng Cathy could see that scores of people had spread out into the garden up as far as the barbecue area and what Bob only half jokingly referred to as his Man's Place, the shed where he had a workbench with a lathe, assorted tools and his accumulated 'stuff' as Roz scathingly described it. She had also told Cathy that when her husband of thirty-five years had been diagnosed as having prostate cancer he had spent an inordinate amount of time out there at the end of the garden, in his shed, 'having a tidy-up and sorting through things,' he had explained to her.

'No man should be without a shed,' Roz had said. 'Its the male equivalent of a woman's visits to the hairdresser, long chats with her girlfriends, an occasional new outfit and in your case a swim, all rolled into one.' They had laughed, but kindly, as both of them knew it to be true. Perhaps Roz's assertion that the shed had saved her husband's life was a bit of a stretch, Cathy thought, but only a bit.

This part of the house was so crowded that they had to more or less push their way into the throng. When Roz, a rather large, but fit looking woman, who was standing at the stainless steel kitchen bench that ran along the far sidewall, noticed their arrival she waved a curry stained wooden spoon at them.

'Over here, over here,' she shouted to be heard, indicating with the dripping implement. She gave them a welcoming hug. 'I'm worried there's not enough food, so I'm doing a fish curry, what d'you think?'

Cathy peered through the crowd to the table along the other wall that was totally covered in platters and bowls of either steaming hot or cold food. Roz was well-known among her admiring friends as an excellent cook. 'Definitely not enough food,' she

CHAPTER THIRTEEN

teased, 'and it all looks so bloody dreary.' The three of them laughed.

'You don't have anything to drink,' she looked aghast, 'you must have something to drink. Oliver!' she raised her voice and waved the spoon again. A younger, male version of herself, squeezed his way between bodies and inquired, 'beer or wine?'

Cathy had always been amused at how alike mother and son looked. Tonight, with her newly heightened perceptions about sexuality, she found herself thinking, 'and yet Roz doesn't look 'masculine' nor does Oliver look 'feminine'. Its strange and complicated, this sex stuff.'

'Beer please,' Steve said, 'and when Cathy comes back to us,' he nudged her, 'she'll have a red wine thanks.'

'Why don't you follow him up to the shed to get it,' Roz suggested. 'That's where we've set up the bar and you'll find Bob out there looking after the barbecue. He'll introduce you to people. I'll come up once I've done with this curry.' She turned back to her cook top.

By the time they joined Bob, stopping several times en route to chat with groups of people they recognised from other earlier Edwards' parties Oliver had furnished them both with their drinks and had gone off to look after other guests.

Bob, who was also rather large, though since his treatment for cancer he was quite a bit less so, was ensconced behind a big portable gas-fired barbecue on which he was grilling steaks, chops and sausages.

'G'day. Glad you made it. Oliver's been looking after you, thats good. He's under orders to serve the first drink. After that you're on your own.' He pointed with a long handled fork to a trestle table on which sat a keg, a sizeable number of bottles of wine and as well, soft drinks. Underneath the table there was a baby's plastic bath filled with cubed ice.

Bob turned the steaks. Several people were standing close by, waiting for the meat to cook. 'Nothing beats a barbecue,' he asserted. Roz is a wonderful cook but a bash like this wouldn't be right without a burnt sausage!.'

'She'll miss her kitchen when you're on the road.' Cathy suggested.

'Perhaps, at first, though the rig we've bought has a decent little kitchen. But I reckon it'll be a relief for her not to feel obliged to produce cordon bleu meals all the time and I'm looking forward to doing a lot of this,' he poked at the barbecue, 'on a campfire, out under the stars.' Bob put some steak and sausage on the proffered plates of the couple standing beside him. 'Dianne and Ray,' he nodded at them, 'this is Cathy and Steve.' The four shook hands, juggling full

CHAPTER THIRTEEN

plates to do so. 'Dianne has been the brains behind the scenes at my place for the last thirty years. Kept us in the black. The accountant.'

'Along with being head cook and bottle washer,' Dianne reminded him somewhat briskly.

Bob's Place, as indeed it was called, was a big auto-electrician's workshop on a busy main road at the edge of Bondi Junction.

' She who must be obeyed.' Bob exchanged a knowing glance with the Connollys.

'Have you had any potential buyers for the business yet?' Steve asked.

'Plenty of the usual tyre kickers and a couple of developers. They're keen to buy it. I'm having a bit of fun playing one off against the other. They only want it for the position. They'll tear the whole place down and put up yet more apartments. Have you seen the ones around the corner?' They all nodded. 'The whole of Sydney is turning into one big apartment block.'

Steve knew that Bob had started the business from scratch and successfully made it grow so that now its shop front spread for several building blocks along the road as well as going through to a back street by including several more blocks.

'You must be a bit sad about selling up,' Cathy suggested.

Bob was adamant. 'No. The time has come. I've been bloody lucky. I got into the business at the right place and the right time. I've worked hard at something I enjoyed. I've had a good run and I'm getting out at the right time too. The cars they produce nowadays, hardly anything ever goes wrong with them. Not like the good old days when they were always needing to be fixed up.'

They all laughed. 'I'm a lucky man,' he reiterated.

Cathy knew all four of them were mulling over Bob's run-in with cancer. As if he could read their thoughts Bob continued, 'Look at it this way. If I hadn't have had that cancer scare I might have been tempted to go on working even though I knew the business was past its heyday. Too stuck in my ways, and not to put too fine a point on it, too bloody frightened, to get out, to let go.'

He turned the sizzling meat again. 'The value of the property would possibly have gone down, glut in the Eastern Suburbs market and all that, and I might have kept on working till I had a heart attack or a stroke.' He poked a sausage, the skin burst and hot fat spattered the grill.

'End of me. At least this way I get to see something of the country and who knows, if the spirit

CHAPTER THIRTEEN

moves me, or we run out of money, I can always start again up north. At least I won't die wondering!'

Dianne and Ray chewed on their meat. A young child, incautiously fooling around in a low slung hammock near the patio, fell out and was comforted by a slew of adults.

'I don't even want to wait until I sign off on a contract for the property. Dianne can handle all that. Probably better than I can myself.' Dianne's expression suggested that she agreed. 'No time like the present. Bit of urgency, I would politely suggest, for us all.'

Steve's body language expressed agreement.

'Cathy and I have decided to follow in your footsteps,' he announced, beaming with pleasure, just as Roz arrived beside them.

'What's this? She pretended to be horrified. 'Deserting Sam!'

Cathy knew she was only getting her own back, in a friendly manner, because Cathy had expressed her own surprise at Roz being willing to leave her grandchildren when they had initially told them of their travel plans. Roz, who until the previous semester had been still teaching, two and a half days a week at TAFE as an ESL - English as a Second Language - teacher, was very involved with her daughter's three pre-school children.

'Touché,' Cathy pulled a face at Roz who gave her arm a friendly squeeze.

Entering into the competitive grand parenting game, Steve told them,

'Lewis and Claudia are having another one.'

There was much good-natured chiacking between Bob and Roz and Cathy and Steve. From the way Dianne and Ray didn't enter into the fray it was obvious to Cathy that they didn't have grandchildren.

'But you're still running behind us,' Roz couldn't resist the dig.

'Not for long. Another one is about to get underway.'

'Sophie,' Bob said.

'At long last,' Roz added.

'No.' it was Steve who spoke again. 'Lewis is the father, but the parents are two women.'

There was a second or more of total stillness as the other four absorbed this information. Long enough for Cathy to register each of their individual, immediate responses. Roz, acceptance. Bob, pleasure. Dianne repulsion. Ray rejection. Long enough also to realise that no matter what they now managed to draw themselves together to say, that very first reaction was their truest.

'Well,' Roz was the first to speak. 'How d'you feel about that?'

CHAPTER THIRTEEN

'Pretty bewildered and upset...' Cathy told them.

'Naturally,' Dianne agreed.

'... at first,' Cathy continued. 'but we've talked it through with them and now...'

'...we think its rather brave and we're proud of them,' Steve finished.

'Its not natural,' Ray spoke up.

'I'd have to agree,' Steve said. 'Not the way they're doing it, at home with a turkey baster.'

Now both Dianne and Ray looked really shocked. Dianne's lips drew together in a thin line.

Bob burst out laughing. 'A turkey baster. Dear God! As if life isn't difficult enough already, for them, for us, for everyone. Do they do it with the lights off as well!'

'Bob!' Roz reprimanded him. 'There's no need to be so vulgar.'

Bob made a pretend feint at his wife with the barbecue fork. 'Don't be so bloody uptight. Here we all stand, four stalwart heterosexuals, thinking the same things. How do they do it. Now we know. With a turkey baster. Why do they do it. I suppose because like the majority of other women, they want to have a baby, to be parents. I say whatever you want out of life, go for it, before you run out of time.'

207

Cathy had a vivid memory of making an unexpected visit to the Edwards' home to drop off some educational research papers for Roz and finding only Bob at home, sitting up at the bench in his shed, assorted screws and nails spread before him. 'What are you up to? she had asked him. 'Just thinking about life,' he had replied.

She found herself hoping that Sandra Forbes would come back with the lab results soon. Whatever they turned up she wanted to move into her future and soon.

'It's just selfishness. They don't think about the effect it will have on the children.' Ray spoke with passion.

His wife added.'How can having two women as your parents ever be as good as having a proper, decent mum and dad?'

'Not all mums and dads are proper and decent.' Bob responded. 'What about that mechanic the police came and arrested at my place last year. Later on we read about him being charged with sexually abusing and physically intimidating his wife and eight year old daughter.'

'Not all fathers behave like that.' Ray retorted.

Bob shrugged his shoulders. 'Of course not. Any more than all lesbians, or whatever they call themselves nowadays, make lousy parents. Give them

CHAPTER THIRTEEN

a chance I say. If you're desperate enough to be a parent that you'll try to do it with a turkey baster chances are you'll try to do a good job. That's about all any of us can do.' He smiled at his wife. 'Anyway I reckon Lewis and Claudia are to be congratulated. Shows they don't just talk about caring for other people's happiness. They do something positive about it. Not many of us get the opportunity to make a big difference. Helping to make a baby. That's what you'd call a bloody big difference.'

More guests arrived for a serving of barbecued meat. As Cathy and Steve tried tactfully to meld back into the general melee Bob called after them, 'Come by during the week to have a look at the rig. It's being delivered on Monday. Bring Sam with you. He'll love it.'

During the next couple of hours Cathy and Steve circulated among the other guests all of whom seemed to have known Roz and Bob either individually or as a couple for many years and talked about them with admiration and affection. The general consensus was that though they would be sorely missed they were doing the right thing, taking off on their trip, and that given half a chance that's what they would like to do too.

'Though I'm not so sure,' a woman with close-cropped blonde hair commented to Cathy, 'about the wisdom of leaving their son to house-sit while they're away. I've heard some pretty awful horror stories about what's happened to people who've done that. Coming back to find the place trashed. Or the children not wanting to move out.

Cathy said to her, 'I don't think any of that would worry Bob overmuch. I think what he feels is, that what will be will be. One door shuts and another one opens.'

'How commendably Zen,' her much younger companion noted.

'Going to the edge can sometimes give people courage,' Cathy turned to Steve who said, 'and perhaps the fact that Bob thinks this house found them rather than they found this house makes it less of a burden.' The couple looked puzzled. 'Haven't you heard that story?' Steve reached out to draw in Roz who was passing. 'Hold on a mo Roz, here's someone who doesn't know the story of your house.' Roz laughed. 'They must be the only people in Sydney who don't.'

Intrigued the couple waited expectantly.

'Well for years we lived in a house only just two hundred metres away on the corner of the next street up,' Roz explained. 'We'd bought it from my parents when it got too much for them and they wanted to cash up and move into a retirement community. It

CHAPTER THIRTEEN

needed work doing to it. We kept tossing up whether to do a small makeover or a major reno. Finally we decided to go the whole hog. We discussed the design and had the plans drawn up and the DA and then the BA went through council. Steve,' she put her hand on his arm, 'organised all that for us. We were a week away from starting into it when the balloon went up on HIH which meant our builder suddenly no longer had insurance and wasn't willing to do the job. We were left stranded. We thought about becoming owner builders and taking out our own insurance but what a hassle that is. So we decided to give up on the whole idea. Poor Bob,' she smiled in the direction of where her husband was still chefing at the BBQ, 'after all the work he'd put into it.'

'But,' her smile became a laugh, 'on the very day we made that decision there was a knock on our door. Eight o'clock at night. There was this couple standing there whom we didn't know from Adam and they said, and this is god's own truth, 'We want to buy your house. We'll give you a million dollars.'

Having heard the story many times before, Steve and Cathy nodded and said, 'Its true.' The other couple were anxious to hear more.

Roz went on. 'They had their cheque-book literally in their hands. They wanted to give us a holding deposit right there and then.'

'And?' the blonde woman prompted.

'We took it! What did we have to loose. A million was much more than the place was worth, to us at least. They left us a cheque for $10,000 and we arranged to meet at their lawyers the following morning. They encouraged us to bank their cheque before that. They didn't even want a receipt!'

'Bloody hell!' the young man expressed his amazement and asked, 'Did you?'

'Too right we did.' Roz told him. 'We went straight from the bank to the meeting with them and did it all legally.'

'So you sold that house but how come you found this house,' the blonde persisted, 'or it found you.'

'Well,' Roz shook her head, 'I know this sounds even more far-fetched, but while we were queuing up in the bank, to deposit their $10,000 cheque , Bob started talking to the man in front of him who told him he was on his way to the real estate agent to put his house, this house,' she gestured around her, 'on the market. We knew the house because we'd walk past it all the time on our way down to Clovelly beach. For months we'd seen this man working on it and a couple of times he'd taken Bob around inside to show him what he was doing. He's German born so everything was done with a meticulous attention to detail. '

CHAPTER THIRTEEN

Cathy smiled with a sense of mounting anticipation as Roz reached the story's finale.

'Bob asked him how much he wanted for it and when he told him $900,000 Bob said, 'can you wait until 2 o'clock this afternoon and we'll buy it from you.' And that's how it happened. Private sales. No agent's fees. We swapped an old wreck for a brand new house .'

'And made a hundred grand into the bargain.' The young man looked impressed.

'A very Sydney story,' the blonde said and they all agreed. 'How come they were so keen to buy your old place?' she asked, 'and have they done anything with it?'

'You tell them Steve,' Roz began to move off, 'I have to serve the pavlova.'

'Perhaps they wanted the old house because it was on a corner block, Steve suggested. 'Anyway they've knocked the old place down, but kept within the floor plan so that technically it still qualifies as a remodelling and they've built an expensive two storey monstrosity.'

'A million for the block and then a brand new house,' the young man commented. 'Must have a bit of loose change.'

It was Cathy's turn and she told them, 'It seems he worked for a international tobacco company, on the research side, and he took early retirement with a big pay out.'

'Hush money,' the man suggested. 'A yet more Sydney story.'

Great pavlova was served, speeches were given, champagne toasts were made. An excellent night was had by all.

Cathy and Steve looked for Roz to make their thank yous and farewells and found her alone in the upstairs sitting room which led off from their bedroom. A comfortable book-lined room from where the daylight view revealed parts of Waverley Cemetery and the ocean beyond.

'Just taking a breather from it all,' she explained. 'Its been a bit full on, getting to this point.'

Cathy nodded with understanding. 'How is Bob? Really?'

'In remission. That's the textbook phrase. In reality physically he gets more tired than he used to, but I guess we all suffer from that. Mentally he's even more positive than he's ever been. He's done a lot of thinking and the result seems to be that he's also more relaxed than ever about everything.

'And how about you,' Steve asked gently.

'I'm taking it one day at a time like they tell you to do. How about you and this other new baby? Really? Have you met the mother, mothers, to be?'

CHAPTER THIRTEEN

'Not yet.' They shook their heads.

'Next weekend.' Cathy told her. 'They're getting married... sort of. It's called a handfasting. They join hands symbolically.'

' Handfasting,' Roz repeated thoughtfully. 'Its a good word.'

The three of them looked out through the window into the dark night. Sounds of merriment drifted up from the garden and kitchen.

'But in the end,' she said, 'we all live and die alone.'

Fourteen

It was Sam who broke the tension and so saved the day.

'Hi Ruby!' he yelled at the top of his voice. He was standing with one leg on each side of his bike and he gave its bell a loud double ring. The small crowd of people collected under the enormous Moreton Bay fig tree laughed with palpable relief. He was parked between his father and Cathy and looking up at her he announced in a loud stage whisper. 'That's Ruby,' When she signalled him to hush he frowned and continued in a voice everyone could hear, 'Her nana is Daisy. And that's Kit. Remember you asked me and I told you, they're getting married.' He spoke the words slowly and enunciated them clearly, simultaneously opening his eyes wide for emphasis, obviously wanting to ensure that she remembered their conversation at Coogee Beach; worried perhaps that he needed to jog her aging memory. 'Remember?' he asked again. Cathy nodded and told him, 'I do, I do.'

He dinged his bell again and waved at Ruby and Kit as they came down the path toward the rotunda. They both smiled and waved back. Now everyone waved at them and Ruby and Kit responded with laughs and waves.

'What d'you think I should wear to this…do?' Steve had asked her earlier that morning.

'Whatever you feel most comfortable in,' she suggested.

'Jeans and a tee-shirt okay then?'

'Probably a shirt and tie.'

'And nothing else?'

Such brittle attempts at jokey conversation were a sure indication that they were both anxious.

Cathy stepped out from the walk-in wardrobe wearing a Purl Harbour straight full-length knitted skirt with matching long-line top in a dark rust colour. He watched as she sat in the corner chair and pulled on high-heeled boots.

'There's going to be a lot of standing around. Will you be comfortable in those? '

'I'm not going for comfort,' she snapped.

'Are you going to wear a hat?'

CHAPTER FOURTEEN

'Steve!' Now her voice was really strained. 'Nowadays nobody but nobody wears hats to weddings. Will you please get dressed. We're starting to run late.'

He glanced nervously at his watch. 'Plenty of time.'

'We have to find parking in the city.'

'Its a Saturday so we'll be fine.'

'Saturday is worse.' She gave her hair, face and teeth a final check in the wall mirror. 'The roads on the way in will be clogged with lunatic mums and dads in four wheel drives taking their darlings to sporting fixtures and music lessons. I'll wait in the car.'

When he slipped into the driver's seat he was wearing a sports jacket over a shirt and tie and she gave him a nod of approval and small smile. As he started up the vehicle was filled with the perfectly modulated and warm toned female voice of ABC Radio's Grandstand presenter. They left it to play, letting it take the place of conversations they didn't want to have.

By the time they walked to the Macquarie Street entrance to the Botanical Gardens Steve was beginning to regain his composure after his verbal run-in with the attendant at the parking station in Bridge Street.

Without even the courtesy of a sideways glance the man had continued talking to a colleague on the far side of his glassed -in enclosure and simply stuck his open palm out towards Steve who was seated in his car on the ramp, well below his eye-level. Only when Steve didn't immediately place money into the palm did he look down and demand,

'Thirty-five dollars mate.'

'For how long?'

'All day.'

'I'll only be here and hour, or two at the very most.'

'Its still thirty-five dollars mate' and when Steve was slow to respond he added in a tone of voice which spoke volumes, as he scratched at his nose, 'See the sign at the top where you drove in. That's what it says, Saturdays. All Day Parking $35 and that's what it means. Half an hour or twelve hours, its all the same. $35. In advance. '

'Bloody outrageous,' Steve spluttered.

The attendant didn't even bother to comment. Having heard it all before and probably at least half a dozen times that very morning. Another vehicle came down the ramp and pulled up close behind them.

CHAPTER FOURTEEN

'You staying mate?' He used the noun in a pejorative manner. 'That's thirty-five. Otherwise go down to that bay there,' he signalled to an empty car parking space at the turn in the down ramp, 'chuck a u-ee and I'll let you back out on the other side.' He thrummed his fingers on the frame of his cash window. Steve paid with a considerable show of ill grace.

From the far side of the pedestrian crossing they could see a little knot of people by the fountain at the entrance to the gardens and Lewis, by virtue of his height, appeared to loom over them. Even at this distance it was obvious to Cathy that he was not happy. As they crossed the road she could see he was talking to a young man in the dun coloured uniform of a park ranger who had obviously stopped them at the gates to the Botanical Garden.

Sam's bike was dangling from Lewis's left hand. His body language was tense and he could only manage a cursory nod of welcome before continuing to talk, unnecessarily loudly, to the official, '...he won't ride the bike, I promise you. I'll carry it. But he wouldn't come without it. Some kids suck their thumbs, some kids carry little comfort blankets, my kid has a bike. Same thing. Won't go anywhere without it. I tried telling him bikes aren't allowed in the park but his mother...' Cathy caught Claudia's eye, smiled and registered how bloomingly beautiful and stylish her daughter-in-law looked, her thick hair piled up and shown off to perfection by the heavy weave collar of her fitted jacket. '...she suggested it would be okay if I carried it.'

Cathy thought, the men are finding this occasion difficult to cope with, and stepped up beside the ranger. Touching him gently on his arm she said quietly;

'We're not going far into the gardens, just to the rotunda at the Rose Garden. Friends are getting married there.'

The young man's whole demeanor changed.

'Aah! The handfasting?'

They all nodded.

'That's fine then.' He lowered his voice. 'Kit's a friend of mine. Congratulations. Have a good time.' He turned to Sam, 'But don't you ride your bike young man,' and was gone.

Steve and Lewis spent the short walk to the rotunda seemingly commiserating with each other about officialdom in all its uniforms but actually each drawing comfort from the company of the other to help cope with their nervousness about the event in which they were about to participate.

CHAPTER FOURTEEN

Ruby and Kit's walk down the path into the shady embrace of the welcoming tree was moving and inspirational. Steve's hand found hers and she returned his squeeze. Cathy could hear people whisper and, scanning the expressions of those around her she was sure that quite a number of them felt like her; joy in Ruby and Kits' obvious happiness uncomfortably mixed with a discernible unease.

Both tall, the women moved, hand in hand with athletic grace and dignity. Cathy's first impression of her grandchild's mother was one of strength and determination. She could have passed as a Sabra from the Golan Heights. Her hair was a vibrant mass of dark shining curls. Steve's description from memory of her as having a wide, generous mouth and attractive smile was entirely accurate. It wasn't until the ceremony had begun that she had time to notice Ruby's sleeveless cream silk draped blouse and long, sage-green, moiré silk skirt that finished just below the knee and went on down to the ankle in a same-coloured lace.

Beside her Kit looked equally dramatic. Handsome rather than beautiful with a well-featured open face. She was wearing a tailored three button dark suit. On the lapel was pinned a simple silver and opal brooch. Her hair, also dark, but short and smooth was groomed back across the top of her ears.

They looked every bit the perfect couple and as the ceremony proceeded it became apparent that a great deal of careful thought had gone into choosing the words to express the sentiments they wished to share with their closest family and friends.

But though this slightly mitigated the feelings of awkwardness and discomfort, Cathy could still feel that a number of the guests would be glad when it was all over

Ruby and Kit were introduced to the guests by a woman, also wearing a well-cut suit over a plain, white high-necked tee-shirt. Cathy immediately recognised her from an article she had read recently in the Sydney Morning Herald. She recalled that the woman was a pastor in a city church, that she had been in a gay relationship herself for many years and that she encouraged other gay women and men to call into question the attitude of the mainstream churches towards practising homosexuals; their inability to participate in the sacraments of communion and marriage as well as their rejection as serving clergy.

She told them that Ruby and Kit had written their own ceremony and about the history and meaning behind a handfasting. Every now and then Sam would ding his bell and the pastor would smile and thank him. Silently Cathy thanked him too for the balance his total acceptance brought to the scene.

CHAPTER FOURTEEN

By the time Ruby and Kit began to speak themselves quite a number of passers-by had stopped to watch the proceedings and the general atmosphere among the guests had somewhat relaxed.

Ruby spoke first. She listed the qualities she had been searching for in a partner, 'honesty, constancy, gentleness, imagination and the willingness to change, experiment and grow,' and how she had found them in Kit. 'I love her,' she spoke up, 'and I commit my life to her. A life we hope will be enriched by the children we plan to have and raise together.' She gave Kit the full wattage of her smile.

There it was again. A slight feeling of unease. Ridiculous, Cathy told herself, when what was being expressed was unconditional love.

A little to one side of Cathy, on the path, a man pushing a stroller stopped and said in a tone of distaste to the woman beside him, who had a toddler in tow, 'Its two women isn't it?'

Hearing him Cathy knew that was how she herself had felt and sounded only two weeks ago. It made her realize how far she had journeyed but more than that, how much further she still had to go.

Kit was a little less confident, occasionally turning to Ruby as if for support. But she too enunciated her reasons for loving Ruby, finishing by promising to do so exclusively and forever.

The pastor helped them to exchange rings and was engaged in binding their crossed wrists together with a gold-coloured, tasselled cord, when suddenly, down the path poured a busload of tourists obviously from China. Their tour leader strode ahead waving a red pennant on a long handle, shouting words of what sounded like encouragement to get a move on.

In a mish-mash mix of synthetic tracksuits and sneakers, ill-fitting suits and scuffed leather shoes, padded jackets and even a couple of full-length cheongsams, all of them carrying cameras and talking loudly in Cantonese, they spread off the path and came to a halt at the edge of the unfolding ceremony. Here they began to take flash photographs of the proceedings almost certainly in the belief that what they were witnessing was a common cultural occurrence.

Ruby and Kit both burst into happy laughter at the bizarre incident, The tourists remained ignorant and moved on. Sam rang his bell. The ceremony was over. The two women kissed each other.

While they signed a certificate, which was witnessed by the pastor and two of their friends, on a small table set up to one side, the guests began to mingle. Cathy noticed that quite a number of them looked somewhat shell-shocked, including Claudia who said;

CHAPTER FOURTEEN

'It wasn't what I expected, because I didn't know what to expect. It was beautiful. Very moving, but pretty confronting too. Makes you realise how difficult it is to be open-minded.'

Cathy surreptitiously studied the other guests and was interested to note that it was not only some of the apparently straight, older, couples who looked somewhat embarrassed to be here, as if they had been caught out at farting or exposing their genitals in public, but a few of the more obviously gay friends too. She was particularly interested in two couples, a generation apart, who judging by their style of dress and physical appearance could only be from the bush and who appeared to be more comfortably relaxed than anyone else there. She was about to move across and introduce herself when Carter appeared, with a tube of styrofoam cups in his hands.

He kissed both her and Claudia. 'What a wonderful ceremony,' he enthused. 'Such courage. I could cry for a week. Sorry about these awful cups but the parks people insisted, no glass and no confetti. Hold on to them,' he gave them one each. 'I'll be back with the champagne. This is getting to be a habit,' he winked.

They watched as he went quickly from guest to guest handing out cups, doing his patter. From inside the rotunda he reappeared, accompanied by Lewis, both men with a bottle of champagne in each hand. With these they circulated among the guests, filling their cups. 'To toast the bride and groom,' Lewis quipped and when Claudia gave a small admonitory frown, he added, 'Got to keep a sense of humour about all this.'

Ruby and Kit completed the formalities although Cathy wasn't sure they could be described as that because, she realised with an unexpected sadness, that real though all this was, it was in no sense a legal marriage.

'Not the time to look pensive,' Steve kissed her lightly on the cheek. 'Let's go introduce ourselves to our extended family.'

But before they could reach the women who were surrounded by a cluster of friends offering their congratulations, Daisy Jacobs, wearing an oversized blue cartwheel hat dripping with brightly coloured artificial flowers, clapped her hands for quiet.

'Raise your glasses,' she demanded.

'Your styrofoam mugs,' Carter grimaced in a loud aside.

'Ladies and Gentlemen…'

'…and everyone else ,' Carter added and grinned at Daisy.

'I give you,' she paused theatrically, 'Ruby and Kit.'

CHAPTER FOURTEEN

'RubyandKit.'
'RubyandKit.'
'RubyandKit.'

The conjoined names were enunciated by everyone; some doing so with more enthusiasm than others; some with obvious embarrassment and awkwardness, still uncomfortable with their mixed emotions.

'Mazeltoft!' Daisy shouted, downed her champagne in a gulp, threw her unbreakable drinking vessel into the air, and stamped it to pieces in the grass where it fell.

'Cool!' Sam was impressed and immediately followed suite, only with a half full cup, with the result that champagne was splashed over his mother's jacket front.

Daisy then produced, from a voluminous, also brightly coloured, plastic shopping bag, a heavily embroidered and fringed shawl of a type which Cathy had only ever seen worn in faded photographs taken of Eastern European weddings at the beginning of the last century.

She drew Ruby towards her and draped the shawl around her bare shoulders. 'There,' she smoothed the old cloth, 'I wore that on my wedding day, your mother wore it on hers. It didn't bring either of us much luck,' she chuckled, 'But its the tradition and at least it will keep you warm.'

'I'm not cold Nan,' Ruby eased the heavy material back.

'Of course you are, your nipples are standing out. Look at you.'

Every male guest had already noticed this phenomenon.

'Nan!' Ruby said with vehemence. 'You really are impossible!'

'Just looking out for your health. Don't want you to catch a chill and die on us.'

'At least not until I have a baby!'

'That's right,' Daisy agreed. 'Then you can pass the shawl on.'

Fifteen

The first surprise awaiting Cathy at Ruby and Kits' reception was to more or less walk straight into Jane Howard. The shock was apparently mutual because for a few seconds neither of them knew quite what to say. The last time the two women had spoken was at a farewell drinks party for Cathy organised by people in her office and held at their favourite watering hole in North Sydney the Friday evening before last.

Within a day of her conversation with Claude Borsellino Cathy had personally told all her closer colleagues of her decision to withdraw her application for the position as Assistant Director of Department and to take immediate sick leave followed by long service leave. To a couple of them she had given a cursory report on her, at that time, still undefined state of health. Other staff members, who only needed to know she was taking what amounted to open-ended leave, she had informed by e-mail.

The first person she had told in full was Pat and after work on that day the two of them had eaten an early dinner at the Blues Point Café. Cathy drank more than usual. Enough that she had prudently decided to take a cab home. They had both become a bit maudlin and teary, reminiscing about their Canberra youth, recalling horror stories from their teaching days and mulling over life's small hits, though Cathy said that she felt the blow to Pat of her son's accident was far worse than anything she herself had suffered.

'So far,' Pat commented morosely. She had drunk enough not to realise the implications of that comment.

The two women promised each other that they would stay in touch through the next six months or so of Cathy's travels and decision making.

They were silent for a while and then Pat had said, 'God it's going to be awful in the office. Jane Howard is certain to get the job now, she's been networking like you wouldn't believe. I wouldn't be at all surprised if she hadn't somehow managed to piss in even the Premier's pocket. She'll be bloody unbearable.

CHAPTER FIFTEEN

Cathy tried to cajole her friend out of her blue mood for she could see that Pat truly felt Jane Howard was not the right person for the job. But even though she was leaving her job, for a long time if not forever, and she knew her long-time friend and her brother's one-time girlfriend was distressed at what she thought of as the almost certain probability of Jane Howard securing the position, Cathy's sense of trust would only allow her to say,

'Hang in there Pat. I have a gut feeling she won't get the job.'

When Pat's demeanour brightened at the possibility of a revelation she simply held up her hand and 'Say no more,' was as far as she would be drawn.

And suddenly, here she was, standing just inside the entrance to the garden flat with a glass of wine in her hand. Jane Howard, yet not the Jane Howard Cathy knew. This Jane Howard had her hair loose about her shoulders instead of severely drawn back and she was wearing, was this really possible, yes, a dress. What was more, a softly cut dress, not a dark grey business trouser suit. The final amazement was that she had legs, was really quite attractive and didn't look at all like the sort of person who pissed in anybody's pocket. Cathy registered all this and at the same time felt Steve, beside her, making as if to move on.

'Steve,' she managed to say, 'this is Jane Howard, from my office.' She smiled weakly, 'I mean my ex-office.'

Jane Howard had also regained enough of her composure to introduce her companion, a woman dressed in a masculine cut suit, who appraised them in an unnervingly cool manner.

'This is my partner, Henrietta.' The suited woman's body language softened slightly when Jane added, 'You may recall my mentioning her to you in the office.'

Cathy had trouble doing so but she realised it was politic to make nodding affirmations.

'So how goes it in your,' she emphasized the description, 'office? Falling apart without me I'm sure,' she tried to sound light-hearted.

'We have a new Assistant Director of Department.'

It was difficult to tell from her manner how Jane felt about this.

'That was quick. Should I congratulate you?' Cathy ventured and inwardly squirmed at her duplicity especially as this Jane Howard seemed so very different from the one with whom she had been accustomed to sparring.

CHAPTER FIFTEEN

'No. Not me. They've brought in an outsider. A man. A numbers man and a political appointee I would judge. We were only told very late yesterday afternoon, after Pat had taken off up the coast, otherwise you would have heard.'

It was hard to estimate whether this soft-haired version of Jane Howard, in her leg-revealing dress, looked wistful, resigned or determined not to let this setback keep her down Cathy was spared from having to work out this conundrum by the arrival at her side of Kit who held out her hand.

'Mrs. Connolly, Ms. Stuart, Cathy.'

Cathy, taking Kit's hand in both of hers, commented, 'Well you seem to know all about me,' and in what felt spontaneously like a natural gesture she gave Kit a kiss on the cheek saying, 'Congratulations.' As Steve did the same Cathy was aware that Jane and Henrietta were pondering on their relationship and how Cathy and Steve fitted in to this scene.

'Sorry to drag you away,' Kit said, 'but I want you to come and say hi to my family. I know they really want to meet you both.'

Steve made their excuses to Jane and Henrietta as Kit took them off and steered them through the crowd, far bigger than had been at the handfasting, that had started to build up in the flat and out into the rambling, somewhat overgrown garden. Here she introduced them to the four people whom Cathy had noticed at the celebration and whom she had assumed, correctly it now turned out, to be from the bush.

'I guess we stand out like the proverbial,' Jock Morgan had a bushman's size laugh when Cathy told them that she had guessed they were country people. When she asked specifically which part of the country he announced, 'We run some sheep on a few thousand acres up near Brewarrina. Top spot, God's own.'

Having introduced them all to each other, Jock and Mary her parents, Paul and Tina, her brother and his wife, Kit left them to get to know one another. But not before giving both her parents a loving hug. She touched the beautifully crafted silver and opal brooch pinned to her lapel. 'Thank you again,' she said.

Cathy watched her as she moved away to make other introductions and noticed that Sam, who she assumed must have arrived with his parents, was behaving towards Kit as if she were an older brother. Not a sister but a brother. He attempted to box with her, giving loud shouts and throwing pretend punches. She had never seen him want to play like this with women, or girls... like her nieces. This was the sort of horseplay he enjoyed with his mates at kindergarten.

CHAPTER FIFTEEN

Kit kept him at a friendly arm's length but he managed to duck and weave under her guard, sometimes launching himself to swing from her arm, yelling with delight when she hoisted him high on her back, supporting him with her arms under his bottom and then letting go so he suddenly dropped to the floor.

'Again! Again! Kit! Again!' he demanded through his loud infectious giggles.

'She loves children,' Mary Morgan broke into Cathy's reverie and she wondered, with slight embarrassment, whether Kit's mother saw the same gender behaviour going on as she did. 'She loves playing with them. Doesn't she Paul? Paul and Tina have got three boys. Ten. Nine. Eight.'

'That's their ages not their names,' Tina assured Cathy. 'George, David and Edward, he gets called Teddy.'

Both the women were small and wiry. Both the men were large and powerfully built. All four had skin which had seen many summers and Cathy couldn't help noticing the sudden line across the top of the foreheads of both men, created by the constant wearing of their Akubras, where suntanned skin met pale skin. Their stance, mannerisms, language, clothing , all set them apart from the other guests. At first glance they could easily be taken as coming from another planet.

'Yes,' Paul agreed with his mother. 'Kit's a top sort. Always been a bit of a tomboy. She'll be a good mother.'

Cathy swallowed and hoped that her smile didn't look too fixed.

Mary said, 'Kit has told us what your son Lewis and his wife are doing for her and Ruby. It's a great kindness. They'll both make very good parents.'

Paul had turned to join in a conversation his father was having with Steve which from the bits Cathy could pick up seemed to be about the severity of the drought, the necessity of trucking in feed and the rock bottom prices for sheep.

Tina had become engrossed with another woman of about her own age to whom she was expounding on the difficult choices she was faced with over the education of her sons. 'In the end it'll have to be boarding school. I shall hate having to part with them. But they need an education to have any choices in life. They may not want to stay and work on the land. Its a great lifestyle but you don't make any money at it.'

Mary fixed Cathy with a countrywoman's direct gaze. 'I would understand if you told me that you weren't wholeheartedly happy with Lewis and Clau-

CHAPTER FIFTEEN

dias' decision.' Cathy didn't contradict her. 'After all it means your grandchild will be raised by two women. By lesbians. I don't know how I would feel about that if it wasn't that my daughter is a lesbian.'

Cathy was surprised and pleased by Mary's directness.

'We've always known there was something different about Kit. Her real name is Katharine you know, like yours only with a K. She got called Kit as a small child and it stuck. Just as well. It suits her. It suits what she is. She didn't have to tell me. I just knew. I knew before anyone else, perhaps even before Kit herself, certainly before her Dad or her brother, that Kit was,' she paused, 'Kit was different. Even as a little child she liked working around the property with her Dad. Working on the equipment and vehicles. She wore dungarees, never wanted to wear a dress. I taught both her and Paul at home until they were high school age and then they had to go off to board. Paul would bring friends home in the holidays, but Kit never did. She was happy to hang out with her brother and his friends and they all treated Kit like she was one of them. They rode horses and motor-bikes, went fishing in the Barwon and hung out at the pub in town.'

Cathy could overhear Jock Morgan regaling Steve with stories of the Brewarrina Rodeo.

Mary continued, 'I reckon men are blind to what they don't want to see, so Jock went on having a running joke with Kit about marrying her off to the son of a bloke on an adjoining property so as to increase the family holding, until one night he went on too long, and she said to him, 'Dad, I'm not going to marry Mike. Or any other man. I'm gay.' He was speechless. So she said, 'I'm a lesbian.' in case he hadn't understood.

Mary remained quiet until Cathy asked her, 'What did he eventually say?'

'Nothing. He went out into the yard put his swag on the back of his motorbike and drove off into the night. He didn't come home for three days. When he came back he just took her in his arms and told her he loved her and since that day we've all carried on as normal.'

Cathy gave her a genuine smile and asked. 'How long has she been living down here?'

'More than ten years now,' Mary told her. 'She finished school and then did her nurses training in Armidale. After that she worked in Coffs for a while. But country towns are hard for these girls. In Sydney, well, it's a big city and anything goes. So it was inevitable she'd move down. She already had a few friends here. One of Paul's school friends had trained as a ranger,' Cathy recalled the young man who had que-

CHAPTER FIFTEEN

ried the entrance of Sam's bike into the Botanic Gardens, 'and she dossed down at his place until she found her feet. With the job she does she's managed to combine her talents; her nursing skills and driving the ambulances, so she loves her work. She enjoys being able to be herself too and of course now she's found Ruby she's very happy. Even though I know she quite often gets homesick for the bush.'

'I'm looking forward to getting to know your daughter Mary,' Cathy told her truthfully.

By now Paul had gone off with one of Kit's friends who wanted to show off her 1000cc Motoguzzi to him and Tina was happily mingling with other guests, apparently enjoying this all too rare opportunity to be sociable. So the two older couples, a quartet who would potentially share grand-parenting rites, spent another half an hour talking about life in the city, in the bush and on the road.

'You be very sure to drop in at our place when you're on your way north,' Jock made them promise when he heard of their planned trip. 'I'll enjoy showing you around.'

The remainder of the afternoon Cathy moved from one group of people to another, finding that many times when she went to introduce herself they already knew who she was, 'You're Lewis's mum,' they would say. Or, 'You're Sam's grandmother.'

Every now and again she would meet up with Steve and they would compare notes.

'Aren't you Lewis's Mum?' he asked her on one such occasion late in the afternoon.

'No,' she told him, 'I'm Sam's grandmother. Aren't you Lewis's father?'

'No. I'm Sam's grandfather. You know what? We seem to have so much in common, you should come home with me.'

They both laughed and Cathy asked him,

'Are you enjoying yourself?'

'I think so. Sort of. At least I'm not bored! In some weird way I feel as though I have to be on my best behaviour. Its rather like visiting your mother.'

Elizabeth had arrived in the early evening of the previous day and had decided not to attend the handfasting and reception even though Lewis had pressed her, on the phone, to accept the invitation. Usually she would do anything her one and only grandson asked of her. But this time;

'I need to husband my strengths. I find big gatherings of people I don't know very exhausting. So you bring Ruby and Kit along to the family lunch on Sunday and I'll be happy to meet them then.'

CHAPTER FIFTEEN

Cathy told Steve, 'I'm glad to hear that you've been behaving yourself. Not pinching bottoms or anything gross like that!' They laughed again and then she asked. 'But have you noticed something odd? Something unexpected?'

'I've noticed a lot of odd, unexpected things,' he rolled his eyes. 'I'm on what could be described as a steep learning curve! But to what specifically are you referring when you say odd, unexpected?'

Cathy drained the glass of water she had been constantly refilling all afternoon. She had drunk no alcohol because she felt she needed to keep her wits about her.

'Well,' she said, 'I thought only the straights, you know, boring, middle-class, upwardly mobile, heterosexuals like us would find all this,' she gestured at the people who filled the garden, 'a challenge.'

'But?' he prompted.

'Well a lot of the others, the gays, in fact most of the ones I've talked with, they're also finding this quite hard to face up to.'

'Why? What d'you mean?' he asked

'Well, partly because I want to know and partly because they put out the challenge for us to be accepting, I have decided to jump in boots and all and I start all conversations by asking them if they have been handfasted, if that's a word, and if they are thinking of trying to have children.'

'Bit in your face don't you think?'

'Perhaps. Though it's the sort of questions I would ask straight young people. The thing is I genuinely want to know, not for any vicarious reasons, but because I need to get to understand this Alice in Wonderland world we've suddenly popped up in.'

'You're braver than me,' he told her. ' I'm just sticking to the social niceties. Safer. Although I have noticed that when I introduce myself they do seem, initially, to be on their guard. Some of them give off a sort of hostility and I feel as though I have to prove that I am tolerant and open-minded. Its a bit exhausting.'

He laughed 'Funnily enough it reminds me a bit of when I was at uni and went to parties and felt like I had to take a puff on a joint to make myself acceptable to all the other puffers. Peer group pressure I guess. So how do they react to you when you ask about handfasting and babies?'

'Surprising. Not what I expected. I haven't found any of them who have made such a public declaration of their love. But a few have said that after today's celebrations they're seriously considering doing so.'

CHAPTER FIFTEEN

'Mmm. Interesting. More peer group pressure. Oh by the way I should warn you that I have made one large-scale social gaffe.'

He pulled a face and shuddered histrionically. Cathy looked inquiring.

'There was this heavily pregnant woman,' he pushed out his flat belly and laid both hands on it, 'she was standing on her own and I began to engage her in light banter. I assumed that she was one of them, if you know what I mean,' Cathy nodded, 'and I was starting to show off my new found knowledge, bandying about words like home insemination when this man appeared beside her and she introduced him as her partner. Then she told him, 'he took me for a dyke,' and burst out laughing. But the fellow didn't even crack a smile. Ooops!'

'Very ooops!' Cathy agreed. 'Especially as when I mention babies to the gay crowd some of them get very snitty.'

'Is snitty some code word I should know about?' Steve looked anxious.

'No,' Cathy reassured him. 'It is my own verbal description of this,' she arched her eyebrows and narrowed her mouth.

'Disapproving,' Steve interpreted.

'A bit. But mixed with envy.'

'Oh,' he frowned and sighed, 'its all very complicated.'

'Yes,' she agreed. 'I suppose what it means is that the gay community, like every other community, is a mix of many opinions. Some of them might even be Republicans!' she teased him about his most ardent political belief.

'That's below the belt,' he gave her a hug and they still had their arms around one another when Ruby tapped them on their shoulders and said,

'Perhaps this is not a good time to introduce myself!'

Smiling and disentangling themselves both Cathy and Steve kissed Ruby on the cheek. She looked pleased with the welcome.

'At last,' Cathy stood back, 'we get to meet.' She noticed that Ruby still had Daisy's old shawl draped around her shoulders.

Ruby apologised for it having taken this long for her to get to them.

Cathy brushed her anxieties aside saying, 'Please don't worry about it. You've had so many other people and things to keep an eye on.'

In an effort to make her feel more relaxed Steve gallantly launched into embarrassing stories about their own wedding reception. 'I was so nervous that when it came my turn to make my thank-you

CHAPTER FIFTEEN

speech I stood on the edge of the tablecloth as I stood up and pulled my full plate into my lap. Then I forgot to thank my Mum and Dad in the speech and to cap it off I somehow managed to be so heavy-footed with Elizabeth, that's Cathy's Mum, when I was dancing with her, that I snapped the heel off her shoe!'

They all laughed and Ruby commented, 'but she forgave you.'

'For breaking her heel yes,' Steve said, 'but for marrying her daughter, which meant her moving to Sydney, no.'

'That's not true,' Cathy rejoined, 'well perhaps half true. You'll be able to ask her yourself tomorrow. You are coming to the family lunch aren't you?'

Ruby nodded. 'I'm looking forward to it. I've never been to a family lunch.'

Cathy recalled her mother's wistful remarks about such occasions.

'Probably because I don't have much in the way of family.' Ruby concluded. 'You're very fortunate.'

'They can be a mixed blessing,' Cathy told her quietly.

They all agreed and then Steve said brightly,

'But you have Daisy. She 's like five families rolled into one!'

Ruby laughed and right on cue Daisy hove into distant sight, still wearing her oversized hat and still gesticulating wildly.

Throughout the afternoon Cathy had made various sightings of the ecstatically happy potential great-grandmother-to-be moving among the disparate groupings, 'like a demented Mad Hatter,' she'd said to Steve, following on from her Alice in Wonderland analogy.

'She's a marvelous woman,' Ruby said. 'Irrepressible. Refuses to let life get her down. I've been very lucky to have her as my Nan. In many ways she's been more of a mother to me than Mum herself.'

'I haven't met your mother yet,' Cathy said.

Ruby shook her head. 'She did come to the handfasting but you probably wouldn't have seen her because she stayed in the background. She hasn't come to the reception. She doesn't feel comfortable with a lot of people.' She pursed her full lips. 'Especially this particular lot. She likes Kit. Most of all she likes her when we visit her place in the mountains and Kit fixes her washing machine, puts up a shelf or gets the fencing in order. But she's had trouble coming to terms with me being bisexual. She feels uncomfortable around our gay friends. And as for Kit and me becoming parents...' she shrugged her shoulders and looked sad.

CHAPTER FIFTEEN

'She'll come round,' Cathy tried to be consoling.

'I hope so. I really do; because I love her and I want her to be happy. Though I sometimes think she doesn't have a great capacity for happiness. Some people don't. I've learnt that. She's also somewhat frightened of life. She's had a raw deal in some ways, bearing the burden of her mother and father's expectations, the father of her children being such a dropkick and then her children not turning out as she would have wanted. But its all in how you look at life isn't it.'

This was a comment rather than a question and Cathy and Steve remained silent as Ruby continued.

'Anyway Shimon, that's my brother's real name and I can't bring myself to call him Carter, and I, we have to get on with our own lives. Children have to do that and parents have to let them go, with love, don't you think?'

Cathy and Steve nodded in agreement and Cathy was conscious of how much she was going to enjoy getting to know this likely mother of her grandchild and what a splendid effort she would put into being a parent herself.

An hour or so later when they were making their way out of the garden and were negotiating their way through a knot of guests, a hand on her arm caused Cathy to turn and come face to face with Jane Howard again who said in a conciliatory, warm tone,

'I only realised today that its your son who is helping Ruby and Kit to become mothers. It is a wonderful thing to do. Congratulations.'

Sixteen

The start of the much-anticipated family luncheon was enlivened by the unexpected arrival on the scene of three whales. Cathy's younger niece, Tanya, was the first to spot them, perhaps a half kilometre offshore and proceeding north at a seemingly leisurely pace.

'Whales! Whales!' she bellowed and scrambled to stand up on the wooden slats of an outdoor chair so as to have an even better view. Sam, yelling 'Where? Where?' tried to imitate her. His chair almost toppled over backwards and only quick thinking on the part of Tanya's sister, Christabelle, saved him from a severe tumble. Undaunted he continued to insist, 'Where? Where?' until the whales breached again and all three enormous backs were spotted by everyone with resultant satisfied oohs and aahs.

Cathy and Steve had been up since dawn and following a wake-up swim they had spent the morning preparing the food and the house for the family onslaught. Digger, sensing the purposeful atmosphere had retreated to a far corner of the deck where he lay snoozing, half in and half out of the shade, at the feet of Elizabeth who, seated in a planters chair under a sun umbrella was finishing off yesterday's weekend-sized cryptic crossword.

Steve had checked the propane gas tank for the barbecue, had the prawns and marinated fish ready to go, had checked the extra supplies of beer, wine and ice in the downstairs fridge and had followed Cathy's check list of to-dos, striking them through as he completed each one. Just why she wanted their bedroom vacuumed and their bathroom floor mopped and fresh towels in place was totally beyond him, but after thirty-five years of marriage he knew better than to query the master plan.

Cathy had her own list she had been working through over the past few days. It included a swag of fruit and salad vegetables for which on the Friday she had travelled across the Bridge to her chosen greengrocers in Northbridge. It was a twenty-minute trip but worth it because they sold such fresh, high quality produce. The location had involved only a slight diversion for Cathy from her routine office to home

CHAPTER SIXTEEN

journey but now she was no longer making that daily trek she could choose the time of day for her shopping and having also finished a large-scale supermarket shop-up she had time for a restorative cup of tea and a scone in the small cafe opposite Woolworths.

She was finding the new luxury of this flexible timetable something to which it was hard to adjust. She repeatedly checked her watch as she sipped her tea, people-watched and ran through in her mind for the umpteenth time the conversations she'd had during the week with Sandra Forbes and the oncologist.

'The results of the tests,' Dr. Forbes had explained, 'show a CIN 3.'

Cathy waited for an amplification.

'A precancerous change in the cells requiring surgical removal. I've made an appointment for you to see an oncologist this afternoon. He is the surgeon to whom I refer those of my clients who require surgery. I trust him. If I needed surgery, he's the one I would choose. You can of course get a second opinion, but whatever you decide to do, you need to move quickly on this.'

'I'll be guided by you,' Cathy responded immediately, 'so I'll go and see your oncologist this afternoon. But I won't be able to have any surgery until early next week because on Saturday we have the handfasting and on Sunday, at my mother's request a family luncheon for which she is coming up from Canberra.'

'Have to get our priorities right!' Sandra teased.

The women smiled at each other and Cathy added. 'Steve and I talked through all you told me about last week, we also had a good chat with Lewis and Claudia and I guess we feel a lot more comfortable with their decision. Still grappling with the detail and coming to terms with the long term ramifications but, well, perhaps we've managed to put it all into more perspective and to feel more positive about the future. Lewis told us that he has banked some sperm with you,' she gave a little laugh, 'well, you know what I mean.'

Sandra looked down at her notes and made no comment; unable to do so, Cathy accepted, for reasons of medical etiquette.

'I want you to feel positive about your own future too,' Sandra looked up. 'The oncologist will tell you about the operation in detail but you know how it is with surgeons, they sometimes have difficulty relating at a non-medical level to their clients. We'll work out some questions now that you might like to ask him. You'll have others of your own. Write them down

CHAPTER SIXTEEN

and refer to them when you're there. Steve should go with you.'

Cathy understood, not for the first time, why she had confidence in Sandra Forbes.

'He'll want to do more examinations, more tests, ask more questions. It won't be pleasant. You'll need a general anaesthetic and you'll be in overnight. He will remove the damaged part of the cervix taking out enough of a piece to ensure that all the cells at the edge of the excision are clear of contamination.'

Dr. Forbes began to write a list. 'For optimum results you need pre-operatively to be otherwise healthy, well rested and in good state of mind. Afterwards he may want you to follow some low level medical regimen; that very much depends on his assessment. You need to be guided by that. Just as importantly you will need some R and R and plenty of TLC.'

Between them they completed a list of questions and before she left Cathy told Sandra Forbes about her decision to lessen her commitment to her career and to travel outback for some unspecified amount of time with Steve.

Sandra Forbes was approving. 'Excellent!' She handed Cathy the list on a folded piece of paper. 'We human beings are strange creatures,' she commented.

'So much so that sometimes we benefit from a challenge and a little set-back.'

Strange creatures indeed Cathy thought as she watched the ebb and flow of people in the shopping plaza all of them seemingly intent only on the business at hand. Each one of them with a story of their own. Seven billion people, give or take a hundred million or so, living on this fragile planet spinning at fifteen hundred kilometres an hour in the limitless void of space. To what purpose their dreams and aspirations. For what reason their fears and disappointments.

'Have you finished your tea, love? The women's voice broke into Cathy's philosophical reverie. 'Its just that we're starting to close up.' Tightly encased in her pale pink neck-to-knee apron, the woman collected the used crockery, gave the table top a cursory wipe with strongly detergent smelling cloth and bustled away without waiting for a reply.

For a further half hour the leviathans frolicked and the lunch was put on hold as the family lined the edge of the deck, passing the binoculars between them for closer views of the creatures. Every time they spouted, breached or displayed their enormous fins or forked tails there was a chorus of appreciation.

CHAPTER SIXTEEN

Steve brought out a book he had on whales and turned the pages of coloured illustrations and photographs with Sam while they discussed the probability of them being Humpbacks rather than Southern Rights or Blues.

'Wow! Mighty!' was Sam's conclusion when Steve told him that the mammals weighed at least twenty times as much as his dad's car.

When finally the creatures of the deep moved on along the coast out of view, the family returned to the main game, settling into their seats along each side of the long table which having been fully extended to accommodate twelve people now took up half the balcony above the rocks, overlooking the ocean.

The outdoor setting was fully laid out with crockery, cutlery, glasses and bowls of salad and they began passing plates of barbecued fish, prawns, salads, wine and bread between them. The winter sun was not too hot and the setting idyllic. Elizabeth, looking frail and pleased rather than happy, was seated in regal splendour at the head of the table while her extended family flowed along both sides, with Cathy at the opposite end. There was an air of relaxed companionship.

Earlier that morning Cathy had paused in her salad preparations as she noticed that her mother, though still with a pen in her hand, had laid the newspaper down in her lap and was staring fixedly out at the ocean.

Cathy walked out onto the deck.

'Read me the clue and I'll see if I can help out,' she suggested bending down beside her mother's chair, though she sensed that Elizabeth was no longer mulling over anagrams. Elizabeth's complete non-sequitur response confirmed this impression

'Have you shown your father's badges, cap and flag to Tom? she asked.

'Not yet. I haven't had a chance.' Cathy told her mother the half- truth. She tried summoning up the mental strength to give her mother a verbal précis of the conversation she had had with Deidre so as to prepare her for the very distinct probability that her son would not be attending this family feast. But her mother was already speaking again.

'I'd like you to bring them all out, for the family gathering,' her mother told her. In a way it would make your father present with us all. I think I'll go and get ready now,' and she began to push herself up on her arms out of the low chair. Cathy wanted to put a hand under her elbow to help her but sensed that

CHAPTER SIXTEEN

her mother did not want any such confirmation of her growing infirmity.

'By the way, Billy,' Elizabeth endowed the name with some distaste, 'told me that he spoke with Steve about the arrangements I have made for my funeral. He had no right to do so but as he has, I feel I can't let it go unmentioned between us.' She looked out towards the ocean again. 'I've written a will of course and I've appointed Charlie Mac as my executor.'

Cathy, who had met the named man on a few of the social occasions she had attended with her mother in Canberra, failed to suppress her surprise. 'You mean Charles MacWilliamson, the ex-cabinet minister?' Her mother gave a smile that afterwards Cathy could only describe as mischievous, and said,

'Oh yes. We go back a long way. Cheryl Kernot is not the first to go astray in the hot house of Canberra. Nor will she be the last. You and Tom could easily have been his children if things had been just a little bit different. Now we're both bordering on senility. So there you go. Life turns on a sixpence.

She looked thoughtful and then continued. 'I've never liked untidiness so I've made it as simple as possible. I've left gifts as well as small sums for the grandchildren and great-grandchild. It will be up to you to see it through because Tom...well,' she shrugged her shoulders and sighed in resigned acceptance. 'You should sell up everything else and just divide the monies equally between the two of you. It may come in handy for you now you are taking time off and going on this trip.'

Cathy had told her mother about the need for her to have an operation, though she had played it down as being a minor procedure. She was about to insist that surely nothing was going to happen to her mother that soon, but Elizabeth turned and fixed her with a steely look, which dared her to make such shallow comforting remarks. Then she gave a firm nod that confirmed the impossibility of Cathy even beginning to approach the idea of telling her that her favourite child would likely not be attending her orchestrated family luncheon.

It was Cathy's turn to stare out at the ocean, though it was with more of a glower than her mother's expression had contained. That's where Steve found her when he came to tell her he had spotted Sophie maneuvering her car in the cul-de-sac and that she would be upon them shortly.

'You okay,' he asked.

'No, I'm not.' He didn't have to persist with his inquiries because she continued. 'I'm sick of being the one chosen to hold the reigns while the chosen one gets to gallivant off.'

CHAPTER SIXTEEN

He knew her so well that she didn't need to explain who and what she was talking about.

'D'you want to gallivant off?' He put his arms around her from behind.

She shook her head vehemently. 'No. But I'd like to feel I would still be held in high maternal esteem if I did. I don't want to be loved because I'm good. I want the option of being loved even though I might be bad.' She shook her head and declared. 'Bugger it.' Then she turned in his arms to face him and said, 'But at least this time I didn't smooth the way for him. If he doesn't turn up he can do his own explaining.'

But turn up he did, just as they were settling down to their meals. Elizabeth had controlled her emotions well enough when Deidre, Christabelle and Tanya arrived without Tom, to graciously accept Deidre's uncaringly casual and harsh explanation of his absence as being, 'because he's taken off with his young girlfriend, so he doesn't even know you are here,' adding with the spite of a scorned woman, 'but I came because I thought you would like to see his daughters. Even they don't know where their father is.'

Though with Tom's timely theatrical arrival it became obvious that someone did and had also told him of his mother's visit because here he was, coming through the kitchen and out on to the deck carrying a huge bouquet of expensive flowers and wearing his most lovable grin that, Cathy remarked inwardly, seemed to bowl over every woman excepting herself. It certainly bowled over his mother for Elizabeth's face lit up with a smile of unmistakable maternal joy and became so suffused with pink that for a moment she looked almost girlish.

Steve, sitting beside Cathy, put his hand over the top of hers where it lay on the table. 'The return of the prodigal son,' was what she had been about to say, but Steve squeezed her hand gently and instead she found herself saying, 'Move up Sam, make room for your uncle Tom,' as her brother pulled up a chair beside his mother. Once she had regained her composure, Elizabeth began explaining to him about her husband's and his father's relics that Cathy had laid out on a small table among the potted flowers at the end of the balcony. There was a slight frisson of awkwardness and a pause in the conversation.

Then, 'Hi Dad,' Christabelle called down the table, her sister did the same and everyone settled back down.

The meal continued throughout the afternoon with people circulating and changing seats so as to pursue conversations of particular interest.

CHAPTER SIXTEEN

Cathy was too busy with the business of being hostess to settle into any lengthy chat, but she did notice that her mother purposefully set out to speak with each person individually. It was only during later shared recollections that they all commented she had not been at all backward in approaching subjects that could have been considered sensitive. It was also only then they also all came to understand she had been saying goodbye to each of them.

'Look at me Nana,' Sam insisted, 'look at me.' Cathy turned from the kitchen bench where she was putting the finishing touches to the deserts to find her grandson was wearing her father's cap and had his badges pinned to his striped football jersey. The shocking incongruity of his young face grinning up at her from beneath the flat topped khaki army cap made her start in horror which in turn gave Sam a fright. He took a step back and assured her, 'It's alright Nana. Grandma gave them to me. Watch this,' and he stood to attention and saluted. Surprised by the depth of emotions she experienced, Cathy still managed to produce a somewhat wan smile and to return the salute. 'Grandma didn't give these thing to you,' she told him then,' she just loaned them to you to try on.'

'No Nana,' Sam protested. 'She gave them to me.' He grabbed her hand and pulled her towards the chair on the balcony where Elizabeth was seated. Alongside her was Ruby. Brusquely interrupting their conversation Sam demanded of his great-grandmother, 'You gave me these didn't you Grandma? Tell Nana.'

Elizabeth smiled, pulled her great-grandson closer to her and inspected the row of medals on his chest. 'I said you could wear them this afternoon and that then you should let your Nana keep them for you until you are older,' adding, 'perhaps you'll become a soldier too Sam'

Sam fingered the medals. 'I'm going to be an astronaut,' he announced emphatically, 'but I don't want to wear this anymore.' He took off the cap and handed it to his great-grandmother. 'It makes my head too hot.' He ran his fingers through his sweat dampened hair and spotting Kit coming out from the kitchen ran off to show her his medals.

Seemingly unfazed by her great-grandson's dismissal of a soldiering career Elizabeth said to Cathy, more as a form of dismissal than a request 'I would love a glass of water.' Before Cathy could leave, she had already turned back to Ruby and asked her, 'Tell me why you want to have a baby,' and Cathy

CHAPTER SIXTEEN

heard Ruby start to reply, 'No one ever thinks its necessary to ask that question of heterosexual people...'

On the return journey with a tumbler of iced water Cathy was stopped by Lewis who was holding Sam in the crook of his arm, examining his chest full of medals.

'Quite a cache,' Lewis commented.

'Yes' Cathy sounded non-committal.

'I had no idea he was so decorated.'

'Grandpa must have killed a helluva lot of men,' Sam commented.

'That's not a good word to use Sam,' Cathy said reprovingly. Sam glanced at her from the corner of his eyes to judge how not good the word was and continued to stroke the medals.

'By the way,' Lewis told her, 'we had a card from Bob and Roz congratulating us on our new one,' Claudia and Lewis were still speaking in code about her pregnancy, not wanting to excite Sam too early on about the prospect, 'and on the possibility of the other. Kind of them to show support.'

'Bobnroz showed me his camping truck,' Sam rejoined the conversation. He had it fixed in his mind that both Bob and Roz bore the conjoined name of Bobnroz and no amount of explaining on their part had managed to persuade him otherwise.

'I rather like it,' Bob had laughed as he showed Sam how the curtains pulled in front of the double bed, how the kitchen sink was covered over and how the cupboards, drawers and wardrobe and bathroom doors were held fast for travelling.

'The most coolest thing,' Sam had assured his father and grandmother, 'is that you can go to the toilet while you're still going along the road.'

Cathy finally arrived back with the glass of water just as Elizabeth asked Ruby, 'What exactly do you mean when you say you are bisexual as distinct from homosexual?'

Cathy tried to linger long enough to hear Ruby's explanation but her mother's formal 'thank you,' had to be taken as her way of saying that Cathy should ask her own questions, seek her own answers.

The table was cleared; deserts were served and eaten. Coffee was poured and drunk. Shadows began to move onto the deck. There was a general lessening in the level of conversation and a feeling that the luncheon was winding down.

Deidre and her daughters were the first to leave. Deidre and Tom had avoided any contact all afternoon and they departed without Tom, though Cathy noticed that both girls kissed their father goodbye and she heard them ask him to call them during

CHAPTER SIXTEEN

the coming week. Deidre was down the stairs but they hung back until he promised to do so.

Lewis, Claudia and Sam left a short time later. Sam gave his great-grandmother a big hug, which Elizabeth, a normally reserved woman, responded to warmly. She took the row of medals Sam handed her and placed them in their satin-lined velvet-coated box, embossed with the Australian Coat of Arms. 'Nana will keep them for you till later,' she assured him.

Kit and Ruby went at almost the same time. Cathy walked with them downstairs and out into the garden.

'She's a remarkable woman.' Ruby commented. 'I'm so glad to have had the opportunity to meet her.

Cathy nodded. It was unnecessary to explain who it was they were talking about.

They then both also thanked her for attending their celebrations on the previous day.

'And thank you too for you gift. It was very thoughtful.' Kit said.

Cathy accepted their thanks and laughingly told them what had happened when she had chosen the gift for them at the Ariel bookshop on Oxford Street in Paddington.

' I'd spent quite a lot of time looking around before a young woman sales assistant asked me if I was looking for something in particular and I found myself telling her that I was looking for a special gift for two women who were starting out in life together. She made a couple of suggestions and then came up with the *Women Travellers* title that I had a look through and thought was perfect because its about extraordinary women choosing to do extraordinary things. I said as much to the sales assistant and I noticed that her manner changed. Then I chose the wrapping paper,'

'Great choice!' Kit commented. 'Those silhouettes of women with perky boobs, sipping cocktails.'

'Then the card.'

'And the card is great too,' Ruby added. 'The nineteenth century painting of two Rubenesque naked women lying on tiger skins being fanned by black slaves!'

'I took them both back to the sales desk where the woman positively beamed at me and I realised that she was doing so because she assumed from what I had chosen and from my comments that I was gay.'

They all three laughed and Cathy said, 'The funniest aspect is that I felt quite good about that. It made her feel better and it made me feel, what the hell! What's the difference.'

CHAPTER SIXTEEN

She left the two women at the gate and met Tom as he was coming down the stairs into the garden.

'I've said my goodbyes,' he told her in a chastened tone. 'She had tears in her eyes. I've never seen that before.'

Cathy found that all she could manage was a quick cool hug.

'Don't be too cross with me sis,' he asked of her. He looked like a dog that has been kicked.

Back upstairs Cathy found that Elizabeth had gone to her room. Steve was clearing the table and Sophie looked up somewhat guiltily from where she was stacking the dishwasher for yet another round.

'I had to let him know Mum,' she said and when her mother didn't show signs of understanding, she explained; 'Uncle Tom.'

Cathy was flabbergasted. 'How did you know where to find him?'

'I know Lynne, the girl he's gone off with. Not well. She was at Monte when I was at SCEGGS and we played hockey against each other. I've seen her occasionally from time to time over the years. I knew she was working in North Sydney and then another girlfriend told me recently that she had seen her with Uncle Tom. So I put two and two together when he went missing.'

Cathy grimaced and sank into a chair. Steve, coming in with a further pile of cups and saucers heard her say, 'What a hopeless case he is.'

'Not referring to your house boy, I hope,' he said and put the crockery down on the kitchen bench top.

Sophie explained, 'No, Uncle Tom. I'm trying to explain to Mum why I told him about Grandma's special luncheon.'

'It seems he's screwing one of Sophie's friends.' Cathy sounded exasperated.

'Mum!' Sophie was indignant. 'I told you. She's not a friend. Just someone I played hockey against.'

Steve put his arm round his daughter's shoulders.

'It was good of you,' he told her.

Cathy grimaced again.

'Thanks Dad, although Mum doesn't seem to think so. But I'm glad I did because it was obviously very important to Grandma. He's a bit of a loser I guess. But she loves him because he's her son. Mothers are like that.'

'She's right you know,' Steve said as they lay side by side in their bed holding hands, too exhausted for any further contact but comforted by feeling each other's flesh.

CHAPTER SIXTEEN

'I know, I know,' Cathy murmured. 'But he gives me the shits.'

They were silent for a while and Cathy thought it was possible that Steve had drifted into sleep. The ocean sounds came through the window.

'Still I am glad she told him and that he turned up,' she continued. 'It completed the picture for her.'

Another silence and then Steve asked, 'Are you going to tell any of them about your operation?'

'No,' she told him, decidedly. ' They all have busy, full lives and I don't need to burden them with a mother's cares, yet.'

'Like mother like daughter,' he said quietly.

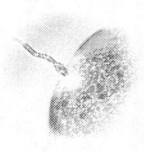

Seventeen

'**Breakfast's** ready,' Cathy heard Steve's voice and struggled back to full wakefulness. 'Time to get up and into it.' She felt his cool hand reach under the doona and grab her toes. 'Another day in paradise awaits.' His voice was filled with happiness.

In the still cool morning air they sat at the small table Steve had set a little distance from the rig, under a huge gum tree. Digger was already lying under the table, in the hope of scoring a titbit or two. There was a spread of fruit and cereal, toast with a multiple choice of spreads, juice and fresh coffee.

'I'm putting on weight,' she complained.

'That's good,' he responded. 'Just what the doctor ordered.'

'She did not,' Cathy countered. 'She said I needed to slow down for a while and eat well.'

'Same thing,' Steve poured their coffees.

AN IMMACULATE CONCEPTION

The operation on her cervix had been successful. Uncomfortable but successful. Not wanting to waste any time she'd had it done in the week following the handfasting and family luncheon and after staying in hospital only overnight had come home to Steve's solicitous care.

It had been a surprise to Cathy how adversely her general health had been affected by an operation that when she compared it with the other procedures women were having in the hospital during her brief visit, was minor indeed.

But when on a routine post-operative visit to Dr. Forbes she had complained of her general feeling of overall fatigue, the gynaecologist had merely nodded and suggested that she listened to the messages her body was sending and take life easy.

'Any operation is an assault on the body. Added to which you've had a couple of other small shocks. Your mother,' Cathy had told Sandra about Elizabeth's preparations for her death, 'and your son's situation.' Dr. Forbes smiled somewhat apologetically at her professionally necessary oblique reference to Ruby's attempts at home insemination. 'Even your daughter's break with her partner.'

'That's a change for the better,' Cathy assured her.

CHAPTER SEVENTEEN

'But its a change just the same,' Sandra insisted. 'and change becomes more challenging ...'

'...the older you get,' Cathy helped her out.

The doctor nodded. 'I keep this,' she opened a top drawer in her desk and retrieved a blank greeting card she passed across to Cathy, ' to remind myself that it happens to us all.'

On the front of the card was a colour illustration by the cartoonist Larsen. It was divided into four squares. In the first a man was walking along the footpath, with a carefree expression on his face. In the second he was at a corner about to step off into the road. Unseen by him, a truck was nearly upon him and travelling at speed. In the third the man had been hit by the truck and was staggering backwards and in the fourth he was lying, splat, flat on his back in the road while in the distance the truck could be seen hurtling on its way. Written clearly on the vehicle, like a brand or company name, were the words, 'Old Age'. Beneath the cartoon was the aphorism, 'The old age truck. You never see it til it hits you.'

Cathy gave a wry smile and returned the card.

'You don't have to dwell on it. Still its a fact we should all keep in the back of our minds.' Sandra Forbes put the card back in the top drawer. 'But you are right some changes are for the good. Less work and Claudia's pregnancy definitely fit that category.'

She stood up and held out her hand. 'Come back for a check-up in six months time. Refreshed. Good luck, stay well and travel safe.'

Cathy had repeated the gist of this conversation to Steve who had often referred back to it when insisting that she rest up while he planned their outback journey. She was surprised too at how glad she was to let him completely take over organizing a house-sitter as well as the seemingly endless myriad details involved in disentangling themselves from their life in Sydney.

Only a month after her operation, Sophie, Lewis, Claudia and Sam drove with them in convoy up to the Blue Mountains to wave them goodbye after a see-you-later lunch on the balcony of Echoes Guesthouse overlooking the Jamison Valley. It was with a huge feeling of relief, mixed with excitement, that they had travelled down the other side of the mountains, out into the flat plains of New South Wales and felt Australia open up before them.

They had road tested the vehicle and themselves by starting with a visit to Kit's family on their sheep property near Brewarrina. Jock Morgan had made good his promise at the handfasting celebration of showing them a good time. They'd gone on wild pig

CHAPTER SEVENTEEN

shoot, assisted with the sheep crutching and been introduced to locals as family, at the bar of The Royal.

When they left there, with promises to return, they travelled south to Cobar across to Wilcannia and Broken Hill, where they browsed through some of the art galleries which had spung up there over the past years. North then to Tibooburra and across the border into South Australia to Innaminka where they were amazed to suddenly find themselves surrounded by a swarm of other four wheel drive vehicles.

'What's going on here?' Steve asked the man behind the counter of the Innaminkca Store, one of the only two buildings in the settlement. The other was a National Parks office.

'Bit of a white fellas corroboree for the Kidmans,' the man explained. 'Family reunion they're calling it. About two hundred of 'em come from all over. Some of 'em from bloody England and the States. Fair dinkum.'

'You mean the Kidman, the Cattle King.'

'Yeh. The very one. Owned half of Australia.'

'Do they all still work on the land?' Cathy asked him. She had noticed that some of the R.M.Williams gear looked suspiciously new.

'Nah, nah. Some of 'em still run a few acres. But most of them are just Pitt Street farmers. Still they're proud of being Sidney's descendents. They're going to run a rodeo here over the next two days and the kids are having fun camping rough.'

'Pretty amazing,' Cathy said, 'to think of that one man having all those descendents.'

'Too bloody right,' the man handed over the bag of tired looking vegetables they had purchased. 'But that's what life's all about don't you think? Children, grandchildren, great-grandchildren and so on down the years.'

She nodded in agreement. Children, grandchildren, great-grandchildren and so on and on. She let the concept run through her mind as Steve drove them out along Cooper Creek to where they made camp. That's what life's all about.

At dusk they put their canoe in the water and watched in awe as the sunset slashed the horizon and coloured the river vivid orange. The next morning they paid homage at the DIG tree and on their journey across the dry flat reg towards Birdsville they camped on a totally treeless plain and were woken in the night by Digger howling in a wild manner they had never heard before. Steve got up to check and found him standing by the dead embers of their camp fire, his muzzle lifted, the hairs along his spine alert, facing out into the moonless dark to where Steve could just make out the ghostly outline and the red reflecting eyes of a dingo.

CHAPTER SEVENTEEN

In Birdsville they had a big wash and brush up in the campsite where they met a World War Two veteran who now spent his life travelling the backcountry in his sturdy rig for months at a time, with only his dog for company. They sat in the pub with him and listened to his stories of escaping from prison camps in Germany and how he finally joined forces with the advancing Russian army.

Then they headed south to Maree where they splashed out and took a light plane flight up to get a good view of the Maree Man. They were welcomed into the nearby campground that evening by a dancing brolga, which lived with the couple who owned the site, having been rescued by them from the dingo fence when it was a chick .

'Its wings haven't been clipped,' the woman told Cathy. 'So it could fly away if it wanted to. But it hangs around here and when I drive into town it flies alongside the truck, waits while I do my messages and then flies back over the top of me. I think it thinks I'm its bloody mother.'

'Is it male or female?' Cathy asked.

The woman shrugged her shoulders. 'No bloody idea. Doesn't matter nowadays does it? I saw on the telly where lesbians are having babies.'

Cathy tried to look surprised. The brolga danced again.

AN IMMACULATE CONCEPTION

From Maree they took the track north, heading for Oodnadatta. And it was on the Oodnadatta Track about 100 kilometres south of the small township, they learnt, if they hadn't appreciated it before, the supreme importance of wheels.

'What the hell was that?' Steve cried, holding onto the steering wheel as a loud 'crunk! 'was followed by a sudden lurch and loss of traction. 'Feels like a blow-out.' He grabbed the wheel more firmly as he eased the rig gingerly to a complete stop. They both got out, along with Digger, to inspect the damage.

'Ohmygod! Look at that. The whole wheel's gone!'

They both stared. The rear drive wheel, on the driver's side was completely missing. Fortunately, very fortunately, the front wheel and the extra back wheel on a lazy axle had been enough to hold up the frame of the rig.

After a few moments of stunned disbelief Steve said, ' No good just standing here. We're a helluva long way from anywhere and we haven't seen another vehicle for ages. I'll get out the jack. You start looking for the wheel.'

There were moments during the next hour when Cathy wasn't too sure that she wouldn't rather

CHAPTER SEVENTEEN

be back in Sydney sitting on her balcony enjoying a cool drink after a long swim at Wylies.

The temperature was in the high thirties. The spinifex scratched bleeding gashes in her legs because she was still in shorts having not thought to stop and put on long trousers and she was in perpetual terror of snakes. This was very definitely snake country and snakes were the one creature on earth about which she was unable to rid herself of a numbing fear. She was frightened not just for herself but also for Digger who had insisted on accompanying her.

After fifteen minutes she had stumbled back onto the dirt track at the sound of an approaching vehicle. It slowed to a halt and Digger raced ahead to guard Steve. By the time Cathy had walked back to the two vehicles she found that Steve, who had been struggling with two jacks, was being assisted by the driver of the other vehicle who, incredibly, turned out to be a car mechanic on a holiday from Port Augusta. He was travelling with his wife and five year old son. Their rig consisted of a regular high wheel-base four-wheel-drive, towing a home-made trailer with tall wire mesh sides in which was stowed an astounding array of sports, mechanical and camping equipment.

'The bloody studs have just sheared right through mate,' the mechanic told Steve. 'I've seen it happen that many bloody times. Those blokes down south,' he said dismissively, 'they always tighten them up with a bloody rattle gun,' he mimicked the bolt tighteners. 'Don't know any bloody better. Up in this country they just overheat mate, to the point where they shear right bloody through.' His hand made a chopping motion. 'Don't s'pose you got any spare studs.' It was a statement, not a question. And he was right. Steve and Cathy felt like amateurish idiots.

'Tell you what I can do mate,' the man suggested. 'I'll take two studs outta each wheel on my trailer that'll give you four to hold your spare wheel on.' He hesitated before asking, ' You have got a spare wheel haven't you?'

Steve and Cathy felt their honour as travellers was slightly restored when they could assure him they had not just one but two spare wheels.

'With four studs you'll be able to reach Oodnadatta. Its only about another hundred.' He looked at Cathy's scratched and bleeding legs, 'Why don't you put some long trousers on and my wife and son'll help you look for your wheel.' His wife, who turned out to be a Frenchwoman from Mauritius and their son, Pierre, pulled on long trousers and boots which they hoisted out of a battered cardboard box stored in the trailer. They seemed to be experienced travelers, prepared for all eventualities. Cathy put on her tracksuit pants and they all began to search on the opposite

CHAPTER SEVENTEEN

side of the track from where Cathy had previously been looking. It was also opposite to the side of the vehicle from which the wheel had sheared off. Again Digger came along for the fun.

Within ten minutes Cathy found the heavy cast metal hub-cap, still hot from friction. But it was another twenty minutes before the wheel was found, this time by Pierre. It too was still warm. It was also coated in red dust and so were the three of them by the time they had rolled it back to the two men. Having completed the task of attaching a spare wheel with the four borrowed studs they were sitting in the dust downing quantities of beer, comparing the cost and attributes of their respective rigs. Steve and Cathy followed the family at a respectful distance to the Pink Roadhouse where they bought half a dozen spare studs for the mechanic and another half dozen for themselves. They also insisted he take a slab of beer as a thank-you from them.

'No need for that mate. But thanks all the same.' the mechanic took the beer and stowed it in the trailer. 'Number one bloody rule of the road mate. Always stop and help out if you bloody can.'

'Number two rule,' Steve smiled, 'always carry spare studs for your wheels!'

The next day they continued on to camp overnight at Dalhousie Springs on the western edge of the Simpson Desert and bathe in the warm, mineral-rich waters. The following night, some 200 kilometres further north, in the darkness of a cloudy night, not far beyond the Old Andado Homestead, they sat beside a small fire and watched as huge sheets of lightning played across the sky. It wasn't until later, when they were brought out of their deep sleep by the sound of fat heavy globules of rain striking the canvas above their bed that they realised they were directly in the path of the storm.

They lay there for a short while but as the sound of rain intensified Steve, shouting to be heard, said, 'We'll have to move out. Its dirt all the way from here to Alice, over three hundred kilometres of it and if this keeps up it will turn into a quagmire further up the trail and we'll be marooned out here for days.'

So, in a mad scramble they collapsed the by now billowing canvas, packed everything up as best they could and found their way back out onto the track. In the dark and in increasing, but fortunately patchy rain, they slowly and cautiously drove towards Alice Springs, which they reached later around midday. There they hunkered down for five days, during which time the rain had become a steady, torrential

CHAPTER SEVENTEEN

downpour that never ceased until finally the town was totally cut off by road and air.

But it stopped as suddenly as it had started and the parched earth swallowed it all up, so that on the sixth day, with the rig bulging with resupplies, they took off on sealed roads, south to Uluru, where Cathy received the satellite phone call she had been subconsciously anticipating with dread.

Sophie's voice was small and tremulous. 'Grandma died early this morning,' she managed to say before beginning to cry. 'I'm sorry to have to tell you, Mum.'

Cathy felt as though she'd been kicked hard in the stomach. For a few moments she forgot to breathe. She couldn't speak.

'Mum?' she heard Sophie's anxious voice. 'Are you there? Are you alright? Mum?'

Her voice came back, though it was croaky with choked emotion. 'Yes my love, I'm here and I'm fine. I wanted you to tell me.' Cathy found herself attempting to comfort her daughter. 'We all knew it was going to happen. She knew herself. She'd said her goodbyes and didn't leave any unfinished business. Eighty-five years is a goodly run.' She swallowed hard and forced herself to keep her voice calm though it still shook. 'Can you tell me how it happened?'

'It was mercifully quick,' Sophie said through her muffled sobs, 'Mrs. Driscoll called me to say that the alarm button had been pressed in Grandma's place. Billy went there immediately. She must have had a massive coronary. She was lying on her bed fully dressed. He phoned for an ambulance but she was already dead. Billy thinks...' Sophie's sobs prevented her from speaking. Cathy waited quietly.

'Billy thinks,' Sophie tried again, 'that Grandma had got up at her usual early hour, showered and dressed, had breakfast because the coffee pot was still warm and had started on the crossword, because...' she struggled with her sobs again, 'because he found the newspaper, folded open on the crossword page, along with her pen, on the side table in the sitting room. He thinks she felt unwell and left it there to have a little lie down and...that was it.'

'Sophie darling,' Cathy told her daughter. 'What a brilliant way to go.'

'I know, I know Mum. In the hospital here they call that,' her voice choked, 'a millionaire's death.' Sophie was unable to speak for some time. Then she said. 'That's all very well, when it isn't Grandma.'

They spoke for a while longer, both crying and comforting one another, making arrangements as to who Sophie should call and what to say to them. Cathy told her that she and Steve would catch the first

CHAPTER SEVENTEEN

available plane south for the Canberra funeral her mother had pre-arranged.

It wasn't until she said goodbye to her daughter that Cathy allowed herself to let go and weep the tears of a motherless child. Steve came back from an exploratory run he'd been making on one of the bikes they were carrying and found her lying on their bed her eyes staring blankly. She told him of the call and he held her gently.

The only remaining flight from Uluru on that day went via Sydney and would have brought them into Canberra late at night, so Steve suggested they take the next day's direct morning flight. For that Cathy was glad. It gave her time to be quiet with her memories and to gather her strength. She was grateful that Steve, recognising this was what she needed, suggested they drive through Uluru National Park the short distance to Kata Juta. Here they walked for four hours in the Valley of the Winds. Occasionally Cathy spoke.

'Mother would approve of us being here,' she smiled grimly. 'Amongst these great geological formations.'

The large rounded female shapes of ochre rock reminded Cathy of the *Women's Dreaming* photograph on the wall of Sandra Forbes' clinic. That in turn reminded her of Lewis and Claudia and of their ripening new baby; of life going on. Perhaps Ruby was also pregnant by now. She knew from occasional phone calls to them that Lewis had been making frequent visits to China but she hadn't asked how that had affected the baby making procedure. At least at the funeral she would see Sam who, she had been delighted to find, was all she had missed during their travels.

Perhaps the recent rain had deterred people for they saw no other visitors. Alone in the heat and the silence, she felt a mix of exhilaration and awe bordering on fear. She also felt extremely aware of the land's total indifference to them.

'It's a good place to say goodbye.' She took Steve's hand.

Cathy was pleased that the funeral went as well as it was possible for such an occasion to go. The immediately disconcerting sensation of everywhere she looked being very green and very full of people was mitigated by Canberra feeling like home and by being with family.

Tom was there, seemingly back in the bosom of his family. Deidre still appeared rather cool, but Christabelle and Tanya seemed pleased to have their father around. There was also Lewis and Claudia,

CHAPTER SEVENTEEN

whose pregnancy was beginning to show, and Sam who looked incredibly grown up in a miniature dark suit and tie.

Of the other people who attended, Cathy knew a few to speak to and a few more by sight.

Elizabeth Stuart had planned her funeral down to the last detail. There would be no open coffin viewing. The coffin was to be white and decorated with a slather of long stemmed red roses. The music to be played as mourners filled the chapel was the Second Movement of Henryk Goreki's Symphony No.3. There were to be no prayers, no religious speeches. Cathy could speak, 'if she liked,' which she did. Tom could speak, 'if he liked,' which he didn't. There was no provision made for Sophie to speak but when she asked to do so on behalf of Elizabeth's grandchildren and great-grandchild, Cathy agreed that Elizabeth would have been pleased. She spoke calmly and with such frank warmth that Cathy felt a surge of maternal pride. Between their speeches a recording of Kathleen Ferrier singing 'What is Life ' was played and as they filed out, another recording was played of Ms. Ferrier singing 'Blow the Wind Southerly.'

As they were waiting outside for the coffin to be placed in the back of the funeral car, Sam slipped his hand into Cathy's and told her, 'I love you Nana.' When she squeezed his hand in silent thank you, he added, 'I brought my new bike down to show you. It's red.' He gave her a wide comforting grin.

The paleontologist had wanted her body to be buried, 'in order to begin the process of decay and eventual regeneration,' she wrote in the notes for her funeral. The family witnessed the lowering of the white box into the red earth. Cathy threw in the first clod on top of the brilliant blooms thinking as she did so about how little space a human body occupies. After everyone else had done the same they left the gravediggers to fill the hole and they went back to the Community Centre in the middle of the area of townhouses where Elizabeth had lived.

The wake, also planned and paid for by Elizabeth, had been organised by Mrs. Driscoll and Billy. Cathy smiled inwardly and had a mute word with her mother about the fact that, though she didn't approve of Billy and his loose tongue, she had to admit that he had done an excellent job of fulfilling her instructions to the tee.

She was still mulling over the irony of this when her mother's executor, the ex-cabinet member whom she now knew had been a 'close friend' of her mother's came out of the little crowd of mostly elderly women and shook her hand. Tom chose this moment to join her too and the executor also shook his hand.

CHAPTER SEVENTEEN

'Your mother was a wonderful woman,' he informed them. He had an unctuous manner and Cathy found herself thinking that she was very glad he had not been her father, the possibility of which her mother had hinted at during the family luncheon.

He made a few more glib remarks of the sort that most politicians would be proud and then said, 'Perhaps we could get together soon to sort out everything. I don't want to appear to be in an unseemly hurry, but actually my wife and I have flights to Europe booked for this Friday.'

Cathy wondered if his wife knew that she had come close to being not the chosen one and was about to tell him that this would suit her fine because she wanted to take a flight back to the Centre, when Tom spoke up in a firmer tone of voice than she had ever previously heard him use.

'My sister is on a recuperative holiday which she has broken in order to be here today. But she is not staying on and I shall be dealing with all these matters for us both. What about we all meet at my mother's townhouse tomorrow morning at nine.'

The executor seemed delighted with this arrangement, staying only long enough to make a few more bland generalisations before making his excuses to leave early.

Judging by Tom's remarks as they watched him ooze his way through the little group towards the door, Cathy realised her brother and she shared the same opinions about their non-father.

'You can leave all this to me sis,' he turned to her. 'Come by in the morning before he gets there and we'll go through and make a list of the stuff you want to keep. I think you should have her Darwin First Edition and anything else you want.'

Cathy went to speak but Tom was on a roll.

'Let Lewis and Sophie choose something that has some sentimental value for them. My girls will do the same. Then I'll have Lawsons come through, give an assessment, pack it all up and have it sent up to their auction rooms in Sydney. We'll get a better price for her things up there. And we might as well get the best we can. Mother would want that. I'll put the place on the market. Billy says there's a waiting list of people wanting to move in here. If there are any problems I can contact you on your sat. phone, but I'm sure there won't be. You just get back out there in the bush and get yourself really fit and well again.'

Recounting this conversation to Steve the next morning on the plane travelling back north to pick up their rig from where they had left it in the campsite at Uluru, Cathy was still full of amazement

CHAPTER SEVENTEEN

'It was a new Tom,' she said, 'or at least one I've never seen before. Did you notice he even looked different? More...I can't put a word to it. Less...less goofy. Let's hope for everyone's sake that the change is permanent.'

'I didn't really have time to notice,' Steve replied. 'I was somewhat swamped by lols.'

'Who's Lols?'

'Lols are little old ladies. Mostly they have outlived their husbands and therefore tend to latch on to any male.' Cathy raised her eyebrows but Steve went on, 'purely because they miss male company.'

'Not a stage of life I anticipate with any pleasure,' Cathy responded by giving him a kiss on his cheek, 'so you just better stay in very good health and confound the statistics.

'I plan to do just that,' he told her and asked, 'So did you question Tom about his personality change?'

'I did.'

'And?'

'He said he felt he'd grown up.?'

'Because of your mother's death?

'He didn't say why. Heavens I hope our children don't feel like that.'

'Like what?'

'Like somehow we're holding them in some form of ghastly emotional stasis and that they can't come into their own until we're gone.'

They were quiet for a while as the Boeing 737 droned on above the outback of New South Wales, crossing, at some purely arbitrary point into South Australian airspace; all the time penetrating further into the increasing dryness of the huge continent.

When he spoke again Steve asked, 'How are things between Tom and Deidre? Has he finished up with the girlfriend.'

'Seems so. Says he's going to give his marriage his best shot. That he wants it to continue.'

'You don't sound so sure it'll work.'

'Well, he doesn't have a good track record does he? Perhaps he feels this now, when the break with the girlfriend is painfully fresh, when he understands Deidre really was willing to go through with a divorce and exactly what that would entail and when his mother has just died. But how will he react in say six months time when the next office flirtation presents itself to his ego? Hard to tell.'

She paused and Steve said; 'Its not just him who'll need to make changes. It's both of them. A man doesn't fall for every piece that presents itself unless there is something missing at homebase.'

She looked at him questioningly

CHAPTER SEVENTEEN

'My homebase is not missing anything,' he assured her gently. 'But don't let either of us get smug. We're both involved in what remains a work in progress!'

She smiled before continuing. 'The best thing Tom said was that they have done a lot of soul searching and hard talking and that they both want it to work. And I do think it's a good sign that she wasn't flashing any new jewellry. Maybe, just maybe, this new Tom and new Deidre will see it through.'

Cathy, surprised to find herself so tired after the emotional roller coaster of the past couple of days, dozed off and was brought to sudden wakefulness by a baby's cry of hunger. At first she wasn't sure if she had dreamt or really heard the sound. Then she saw the woman in the window seat across the aisle put her baby to her breast.

'You woke the baby up with your snoring,' Steve told her with a little smile.

'I don't snore.'

'No I know. Women don't snore. And they don't fart.'

'Absolutely correct! How much longer do we have to go?'

'About another half hour. Gives you some feeling for the size of the place, when you think we've been going at nine hundred kilometres an hour for more than two hours.'

She tried dropping back into sleep but couldn't find a comfortable enough position. As she was still restless he asked her, 'Did you talk to Lewis about Ruby and Kits' baby?'

'Briefly. They've had a few tries.'

He grimaced. 'Sorry. Its still hard to think about the details.'

'I know,' she nodded. 'But so far nothing has taken.'

'Did you discuss the fact that failure rates for home inseminations run so high?'

'A bit, but they are trying to hold on to being positive.'

'So they're not thinking about going to the clinic?'

'Not yet. They plan to go on as they are until the end of the year at least.'

Just then the flight attendant came by to check that seat belts were securely fastened, tables stowed and chair-backs in an upright position and they began their descent to Uluru.

Eighteen

As usual it was the birds that woke her. She leant up on her elbows, rested her head on the back of her clasped hands and looked out through the plastic window in the canvas cover over her head to watch as a huge flock of sulphur-crested cockatoos tore through the sky screeching vociferously and apparently cursing as they went.

The silence they left behind seemed by contrast to be even more intense and Cathy snuggled back down into the double bed under the doona, luxuriating in her favourite time of day. As she lay there she could hear the sounds of Steve moving around outside; going through his early morning routine of shaving followed by breakfast making.

They had returned from Canberra to find their rig, where they had left it, in the campground at Uluru, and Cathy, climbing up the little ladder to their bed, had exclaimed, 'I feel like a joey must when it hops back inside its mother's pouch!'

The next couple of days were spent walking in the area and around the base of the enormous, monolithic stone mound, stilled by its powerful emanations of spiritual power. In deference to the Aboriginal community's suggestions, they had not taken photographs, nor climbed up the side. Though the hundreds of tourists who were disgorged daily by the busload ignored these polite requests on the signboards, hauling themselves up the rock-face, hanging on to the safety chain, chattering loudly and snapping away like the most avid paparazzi.

But at sunset, at the special viewing area set up half a kilometre back from the rock, the awesome splendour of Uluru stilled the voices, though not the camera shutters, of even the most insensitive or jaded visitor. Imperceptibly, the colour on the rock face changed from a blinding deep ochre, through pale pink, a startling yellow to mud brown and then black, slow fading away until it left just the merest shadow of itself against the rich navy-blue sky. Then the stars began to show, a crescent moon hung low, a slight wind riffled the spinifex and Cathy shivered with the land.

CHAPTER EIGHTEEN

On their way back to Alice Springs, they reclaimed a very disgruntled Digger from the kennels where they'd had to board him because he was not welcome in any national park. He punished them by remaining distant to them for several hours, eventually won over by a meal of expensive chopped fresh meat. During the next few days they spent an evening listening to a concert of bush songs and traveled out on the bitumen loop track, much despised by locals but loved by those operating tourist-dependent businesses, to Albert Namatjira's land and the Hermannsburg Community in the shadow of the West MacDonnell Ranges.

By now they felt it was time to test themselves a little further and cross the thousand kilometres of the Tanami Desert to Fitzroy Crossing. They fueled up before they left Alice and again, after two hundred kilometres, at the Tilmouth Wells Roadhouse. But when, after a further hundred kilometres, they turned the short distance off the track into the Yuendumu Aboriginal community, hoping to top up yet again, they found they had driven into mayhem.

A white policeman held up his hand to prevent them from parking their rig and walked across to inform them, 'Been a bit of trouble here mate. Better you don't stop off. Which way you headed?'

After Steve had told him he said, 'Next fuel is at Rabbit Flat, just over three hundred Ks. You got enough on board for that?'

Digger, roused from his sleep on the back seat silently eye-balled the police officer who returned the favour.

Steve nodded. 'Yes.'

'Beaut. Let's see now, today's ...' he paused.'

'...Wednesday,' Steve told him.

'Right. They're only open Tuesdays, Wednesdays, Thursdays. So you'll have to get there sometime tomorrow, unless you want to hang about for a few more days. You got enough water to do that? Beaut,' he said again when Steve assured him that they had sufficient water and food supplies for a week. 'After Rabbit Flat the next fuel is at Carrunya and that's a further three hundred and fifty.'

Steve thanked him for his advice and Cathy asked,

'So what's going on here?'

The policeman shook his head. 'You wouldn't want to know about it mate. Same shit. Coupla kids smashed their way into the generator room of the store.'

He gestured with his thumb over his shoulder at an ugly, squat, galvanised iron shed with heavily

CHAPTER EIGHTEEN

barred windows. When Cathy and Steve looked puzzled he explained,

'Its a petrol generator. The only petrol on the settlement. They're sniffers. Addicts. Brains all eaten up.'

The mightily reinforced door to the shed was open and the sounds of raised voices and wailing emerged.

'Are they alright?' Cathy asked.

The police officer looked at her with the contemptuous pity those at the coalface reserve for all others who are not in the know. He shook his head and assured her, 'No mate, they're not. So, like I said, it's a good idea if you keep moving.' As an afterthought he added, 'Please.'

That night they camped among metre-high termite mounds and the next day filled up at Rabbit Flat. Following that they crossed just over the border into Western Australia and decided to risk a visit to another Aboriginal community; this time at Balgo where they were relieved to find all was calm.

Following signs that read, Art Centre, they walked into an Aladdin's Cave of magical art. The walls were covered with fantastical Dreaming stories created by people from the settlement, some of whom were painting away while sitting cross-legged on the floor.

Cathy and Steve talked with the community art coordinator, a young white woman called Astrid who was from Melbourne and who invited them to stay overnight, putting up their rig outside her demountable home. After dinner they set up collapsible camp chairs on the dry red earth in the cool and then stayed up talking half the night.

Perhaps it was the pure desert air and majestic night sky above, the utter silence, or the sensation of being cut off from the norms of society, rather like passengers on a long sea voyage; for whatever reason, Cathy found herself talking to Astrid about Lewis and Claudias' decision to father Ruby and Kits' baby.

'What a great thing to do,' was Astrid's reaction. 'He must be a very special person and they must be a very together couple. How great,' she said again, 'You must be proud of them.' She was quiet for a moment and then added, 'Perhaps that's the answer for me. Not that I'm gay. But finding the right man, who's ready to commit, is very difficult. I'm thirty-five and running out of time. Being a single mother wouldn't be my ideal choice but...' Astrid sighed.

Cathy thought of Sophie.

CHAPTER EIGHTEEN

After leaving Astrid and successfully negotiating the Tanami they had travelled on via Fitzroy Crossing to Derby where they had stayed a while in the small community to have one of their periodic full-scale wash and brush-ups, as well as having the truck checked over and serviced. They ate every night at an unexpectedly good restaurant near the pier where they swapped tales with other travellers, many of them similar in age to themselves.

'Grey nomads is what we're called,' a large man in his late sixties informed them, 'spending our children's inheritance.'

'I would prefer to be described as an eleutheromaniac,' Steve said.

'Is that something like a nymphomaniac,' the man asked hopefully.

'Sort of,' Steve grinned. 'It's someone with a mad passion, not a man passion. A mad passion for freedom.'

'Eleutheromaniacs Rule. O.K!' Cathy shouted a couple of days later, above the rattles of the rig and its contents as Steve kept going at a steady sixty kilometres an hour to stay across the top of the sharp corrugations and patches of treacherous fine red bulldust of the Gibb River Road. Digger, who had been trying to balance on all four feet in the back seat, gave up this impossible task and settled down with a groan.

'Aren't you glad you suggested we come here?' teased Steve, who also had to raise his voice to be heard 'Only seven hundred kilometres to go.' He grinned with boyish enthusiasm.

But inexorably the Gibb River Road took its toll. A small hairline fracture developed in the chassis that had necessitated a welding repair job they had done by a helpful station owner. The man had oxyacetylene welding gear as part of a wide range of equipment giving him the total self-sufficiency he needed so far from any other assistance.

'And to think,' said Cathy, 'I get the repair man in just to adjust the fan belt on my clothes dryer!'

While downing huge mugs of thirst-quenching tea in the station-owner's workshop cum office, Steve and Cathy noticed a selection of enlarged colour photographs of Aboriginal rock and cave paintings.

'Bradshaws!' Steve exclaimed. The fine boned ochre figures with elegant hairdos and complex ankle and elbow jewelry they had first seen in tourist brochures back in Sydney, danced again. 'Do you sell these? They're for sale?'

'Yeah mate,' the man seemed less than enthusiastic, 'I got scores of 'em on my place. Probably hundreds more I've never even seen. I sell them, but

CHAPTER EIGHTEEN

they're a bloody curse. Got all these bloody uni types from down south and out west and from all over the world wanting to get in here and look at 'em. And now I got the blackfellas threatening me if I let them. Mate, like I said, they're a bloody curse.'

'Why do the Aborigines not want the paintings looked at?' Cathy asked.

'Why d'ya bloody think, mate? 'Cos when they were first discovered by this fellow called Bradshaw, back in the eighteen hundreds, everybody thought they were done by the Aborigines and they were sort of accepted as proof that the Aborigines were the first people to live here. Then everybody sort of forgot about them,' he took a swig from his mug of tea.

'Then in nineteen seventies this bloke called Walsh came out from Queensland and started photographing them and people who saw the photographs started to suggest that they didn't look very Aboriginal, leastways not like the Aborigines we know nowadays. They were able to carbon-date a few of the paintings... where they'd been painted over organic remnants and this showed that they've been here longer than the present people claim to have been. So that puts them in a bit of a bind. It means they were done by people long before the present tribes were here. So it means the Aborigines were not the bloody original inhabitants. They pushed others out and took over.'

'Same as it ever was,' Steve suggested. 'All over the world, all through history.'

'Yeah mate,' the man agreed. 'But it isn't politically correct. So like I say, the paintings are a bloody nuisance. I've taken these photos, and I sell 'em, but now I've stopped people tramping all over my place to look at 'em.' He paused, at Steve's obvious disappointment, then smiled. 'But you can take a walk out along the track behind the dunny and check some of 'em if you like, while I finish up with your chassis.'

It was after breakfast, a few days later when they had taken their second cup of coffee with them to the river, clambered across some large boulders to near the middle, and then sat with their feet in the clear water, watching it dash and chortle its way south, that Steve asked;

'So. Today's The Day then is it?' His voice thick with anticipation. 'The Day of The Falls!'

Now that they were so close to this mythical goal it seemed a pity to hurry matters. Cathy lifted one foot out of the river and letting the water drip from her toes watched as the circles they created were swirled away and swallowed up in the mass of moving water.

CHAPTER EIGHTEEN

'Or, we could put the canoe in and paddle upstream for a bit,' Steve suggested, though sounding a little disappointed and when she continued lazily marvelling at chaos theory illustrated by her toe drips, he added, 'there again we could just lie around in the shade and read. Do you want me to decide?'

'Yes. You decide. I feel too lazy to do even that.' She gave him a sunny smile. She felt her body humming with the pure pleasure of living.

It had been like that since they took to the road. Steve made suggestions and then she deferred to his decisions. What a relief it was to slip out of gear and coast along in neutral.

'The Falls it is then,' Steve announced with determination.

They waded across the river in their bathers, with their boots slung around their necks, clothes held high. Steve carried a daypack crammed with a large-scale map, compass, sun-block, a camera and sandwiches and they each had a full water bottle. Cathy's pack held the satellite phone.

'Bring it along,' Steve had suggested, 'and we'll call someone from up there just to let them know we've achieved our final objective.'

Though it was still only eight in the morning the temperature was already edging into the high twenties.

On the other side they struggled back into their clothes and walked side by side through the coarse spinifex, skirting the rough faced boulders, in companionable silence. During the weeks, that had turned into months, Cathy had noticed they talked less, but communicated more. Quite often Steve would begin to talk about a subject she had been silently exploring herself. Or it happened the other way around. For the first time in more than a quarter of a century they had time to range far and wide in their contemplations without the time constraints or obligations of family, work and a social life.

Over the next hour the heat increased until at last, clambering up onto a long stretch of bare black rock, they looked down into a ravine cut by the river flowing beneath them. From where they stood the plateau, devoid of any sign of other human beings spread off into the far distance until it melded into an indistinct blue horizon. Carefully they climbed down, glad for the protection their walking boots and long trousers gave them. They were nearing the bottom when from a little cluster of almost leafless thorn trees a

CHAPTER EIGHTEEN

couple of screaming parrots flew out in a brilliant flash of colour.

From there it was only a short scramble through the river-crushed black stones to the edge of the water which tumbled and fell in a series of small and large waterfalls.

They took off their footwear and clothes and tested the water temperature.

'Ooh! Cold!' Cathy pronounced.

'Its just feels cold because we're hot,' Steve assured her.

She laughed. 'You know Steve, that remark could be said to sum up your attitude to life.'

He splashed her.

'And I was going to say that's why I love you,' she splashed him back.

They played in and out of the water for quite some time, venturing further and further along the river, trying out first the little and then the bigger waterfalls; becoming braver and less cautious and all the time aiming towards a waterfall that plunged perhaps eight metres off a rock shelf to fall into a deep pool.

When they finally made it to this pool they found they could forge their way through the falling heavy curtain of water into a big air pocket behind from where they could look back out at the river.

AN IMMACULATE CONCEPTION

'No one can see us in here,' Steve yelled to be heard above the din of the water. He looked immensely pleased with himself.

They frolicked in and out of the falling water, letting it pummel their heads, faces and bodies for a little while and then swam back to the bank where Steve suggested,

'Let's get up to the top and jump in.'

To reach the jutting shelf they would have to negotiate their way boulder by boulder across an arm of the river.

'Looks like a perfect place for lunch and a bit of a carry on,' Steve gave a lewd grin.

'Rather public, don't you think?'

'Definitely,' Steve agreed. 'We'd be spotted by all those people who we've seen pouring off the tourist buses! Come on, let's do it,' and he began gathering up their assorted belongings.

After leaping and scrambling to the far side they carefully pushed their way through a few more thorny bushes and up the rock face to the top where another arm of the river made its way down to the ledge prior to its fall. There they stood on the very edge of the overhanging lip and squinted at where the fall of water plashed into the river throwing up spray and fume as it landed.

CHAPTER EIGHTEEN

'Phew! It looks a lot further down from up here than it did from over there.' Cathy sounded anxious.

'Ah, but it isn't!' Steve tried to reassure her.

'Umm,' she sounded unconvinced. 'I'll let you jump first.'

'You promise you'll follow?'

She hesitated before giving a timorous, 'Yes.'

Steve walked to the edge again and curling his toes with anticipation he spread his arms wide and yelled, 'Mitchell Falls. We made it.'

Just at that moment the satellite phone, wrapped in Cathy's discarded clothing, inside her daypack, emitted a piercing sound.

Steve teetered forward, but waving his arms to regain his balance, yelled, 'Bloody hell, what timing,' and stepped back from the edge as Cathy rummaged through her possessions and dragged out the squawking device.

'Hello. Hello,' she spoke and on hearing Sophie's voice asked anxiously, 'Hello darling. Is everything alright.'

Steve came to squat down beside her.

'Yes, yes we're fine,' she waited while Sophie spoke and then told her, 'we're at Mitchell Falls. Its in the Kimberley.' She paused again. 'The Kimberley, darling. Look it up in the atlas.' Something else was being said and Steve waited patiently while Cathy made a little face at him and said, 'Okay put her on.' She put her hand over the mouthpiece and told Steve, 'Ruby's with her and wants to speak.'

There was a longer pause, during which Cathy had time to register that this was one very bizarre scene. Two naked people squatting down on a rock face above a waterfall, in a wilderness area surrounded by hundreds of kilometres of empty land, shouting into a piece of equipment which made it possible for them to be heard almost five thousand kilometres away.

'Yes, yes, I can hear you Ruby.' Cathy spoke into the machine, 'in fact your voice is so clear it's just like you're here with us.' Cathy stopped speaking and in a second or two her face split into a huge smile, she turned to Steve and announced, 'she's pregnant! Two months.'

Steve laughed loudly and shouted, 'Congratulations!' in the direction of the mouthpiece. There was more conversation from the other end before Cathy told Steve, 'She wanted us to be the first to know, after Lewis and Claudia and Sam of course. Now Sophie wants to...hello darling...yes... that's right, the Kimberley. Well we're sort of half way between Derby and Kununurra...I have no idea darling. I guess Kununurra has some sort of airport. It must have because it's close to Lake Argyle. Why?' Again she listened to

CHAPTER EIGHTEEN

what was being said at the other end. 'I see. You're planning on flying up.' She made a less than enthusiastic face at Steve, who responded with a similar reaction. 'Yes. Yes darling that's fine...you want to bring who?' Now Steve actually scowled. 'Dave who?... I see...we haven't met him...you're getting married...the father of your baby...you mean...you're pregnant! Two months pregnant too!'

The satellite phone chose that moment to suffer an unexplained hiccough and all communication was lost.

For a few seconds Cathy and Steve stared at each other. Then Steve stood up, pulled Cathy up after him and holding her firmly by the hand ran with her to the lip from where they both leapt out into the void.

'Here we go!' Cathy yelled.

ABOUT THE AUTHOR:

Trish

....has been a journalist, a radio and TV producer and presenter, as well as an author, for more than forty years. She has written several fiction and non-fiction works, as well as co-authoring five non-fiction books with Iain Finlay.

A co-founder and Associate Producer of the internationally successful science programme for television, Beyond 2000, she has travelled, lived and worked on every continent. In recent years she and Iain have worked as volunteers with the Voice of Viet Nam radio network helping broadcasters there improve their English language programming. In 2008, an epic 21,000-kilometer five-month journey from Singapore to Venice, through south East Asia, across China and Central Asia by rail and other public transport, became the subject of their most recent book : The Silk Train', which is also available through our website at: www.highadventureproductions.com.

The two of them have recently embarked on the challenging task of wrenching back the ownership of all their titles, written solo or together and are having a deal of enjoyment in establishing an e-publishing company, by which they hope to make all their previously published and unpublished, as well as soon to be written titles available to a wider public. To this end, all of 2010 was spent doing research in Asia, including Viet Nam, China, Mongolia and six months in Laos.

She and Iain have children and grandchildren and, when not traveling, live in Australia on the far north coast of New South Wales.

Read about other titles by Trish Clark:

*ANDREA
*AUSTRALIAN ADVENTURERS
*MOTHERHOOD
*CHILDREN OF BLINDNESS

with **Iain Finlay**

*AFRICA OVERLAND
*SOUTH AMERICA OVERLAND
*ACROSS THE SOUTH PACIFIC
GOOD MORNING HANOI
THE SILK TRAIN

Titles marked with an asterisk were originally published under Trish's previous name, Trish Sheppard.

ANDREA
Trish Clark

Ahead of the kiss and tell pack by several decades *Andrea* was a close intimate of European royalty and silent-screen Hollywood stars as well as Australian politicians and socialites. She also spent four character-building years in a Japanese prisoner of war camp.

At the time of its publication her no-holds-barred biography caused a legal flurry at the highest levels. Despite demands for its publication to be banned, it has gone on to become an established social history of a time when live radio was the power domain and Andrea was its Queen. 'He was up me like a rat up a rope,' is just one of her earthy comments about an Australian Prime Minister.

Now, with all her personal papers stored in their own archive at the Library of NSW its time to re-read her story and be amazed how little has changed when it comes to Sex, Money and Politics.

(Illustrated. Available 2011)

MOTHERHOOD
Trish Clark

Fifteen women living through the various stages of motherhood from pregnancy to the anticipation of an empty nest, reveal their innermost desires and fears. While dealing with the unexpected blows of early widowhood, an offspring's physical incapacit, or even a child's death from drug addiction, they unveil the determination and courage that is at the core of their chosen lifelong role.

Strung along the thread of the author's own experiences their survival mantra, at a time when the choice for motherhood is no longer a natural given, is the feeling that there is only one thing worse than having children and that is not having them.

(Illustrated. Available 2011)

CHILDREN OF BLINDNESS
A Brutal Exposé of Bigotry and Prejudice in Outback Australia
Trish Clark

Causing a storm of controversy on first publication, Children of Blindness, a powerful drama set in the small, fictional, but archetypal outback country town of Woongarra, depicts with stunning force, the violent interaction of a small group of people; black and white, over a period of little more than a week, in which three of them die.

Based on actual events at the time, this searing novel opens with Dougo Foster returning from six months in prison to find his children taken into care because of gross neglect by his drunken, pregnant wife, Flo. His attempts to get them back are the central thread along which the story unfolds, revealing layer upon layer of alcohol-fuelled degredation, violence and hope- lessness for the indigenous community, amidst virtual total disapprobation and contempt from most of the white residents of the town. But fortunately not all.

And then there's the law; the compassionate cop, in con- trast to his red-neck colleague, who regards all aborigines as hopeless bloody boongs. There is, however, little either can do when a series of events combine to tip the teetering township over the edge, into a night of unremitting horror.

(Available now: <highadventureproductions.com>)

AUSTRALIAN ADVENTURERS
Trish Clark

What drives a person to purposely place themselves beyond the comfortable, safe borders of the known; to push on further, to the risky edge and perhaps even over it?

Is there some intangible physic payment for placing yourself in physical jeopardy? Is that reward so addictive that it cannot be resisted as it grows to be a compulsion beyond family, friends, financial reward, even life itself.

Twenty *Australian Adventurers,* of all ages, share the passion that drives them to film sharks in the wild, climb Everest or become Australia's first aviatrix. To solo sail or to helicopter solo around the world. To voyage alone in the Antarctic or to recreate the 4000-kilometer open boat voyage of the Bounty mutineers. To be determined to hold the world hang gliding records for both height and distance at the same time, or to be the first to canoe right around the Australian continent. To put grandmotherhood on hold in order to become a backpacker, or to join the wartime resistance. Stories about those who dare ...to delight and challenge those who stay at home.

(Illustrated. Available 2011)

TRAVELING WITH CHILDREN

You'd love to travel to remote and exotic places but...you have kids. So? Why let that stop you? You're worried about their education...think you should wait. Don't!

Iain and Trish didn't. They made three big journeys through some of the toughest territories in Africa, North and South America and the South Pacific with their two young children. Using public transport; buses, trains, trucks, trading vessls, sometimes hitching, each of them shouldering their own backpack, they spent months at a time on the road.

Spread over period of just on four years, their travels took them first from Capetown to Cairo. Eighteen months later they journeyed overland from Canada to Tierra del Fuego, at the bottom tip of South America and within another year and a half, they island hopped across the South Pacific from Chile to Australia.

Not only did they survive to write the books, which also look at the history, politics and way of life of the countries through which they traveled, but, with the passing of the years they know their travel adventures truly sealed an on-going adult friendship with their children.

(All titles illustrated and available 2011)

AFRICA OVERLAND
Iain Finlay & Trish Clark

Capetown to Cairo! A magical phrase...the journey of a lifetime. Around 12,000 kilometers, nine countries, four months on the road with nothing booked or arranged in advance. With their two children; a son aged eight and daughter nine, carrying their own back-packs and often sleeping in rough circumstances (like in the back of a truck laden with copper ingots), Iain, Trish and the kids get to see: Kruger National Park, Victoria Falls and travel on the TanZam railway. They experience the vast herds of game in Serengetti, Lake Manyara, Ngorongoro and Amboseli, go to the source of the Blue Nile in Ethiopia, travel on 'Kitchener's Railway' across the Nubian Desert from Khartoum to Wadi Halfa, Aswan and the great temples of the Nile Valley... all the way down to Cairo and the Pyramids.

And the kids did travel projects the whole way!
Projects that were the envy of their classmates.

SOUTH AMERICA OVERLAND
Iain Finlay & Trish Clark

This incredible journey includes much more than just *South America*. It starts in Canada as Iain, Trish, their ten-year-old son and daughter, aged eleven, set out in a blizzard that covers most of the US, to deliver a car cross-country to San Diego. Then they travel by train and bus through Mexico, Belize, Guatamala, El Salvador, Honduras, Nicaragua and Costa Rica to Panama. Along the way they visit the great Aztec and Mayan temples of Tenochtitlan, Palenque, Tikal and many others.

Then on to Ecuador and Peru, where they puzzle over the mysterious lines in the Nazca Desert and visit the fabled Lost City of the Incas at Machu Picchu. Across the Andes, on the Amazon River headwaters, at Pucallpa and down-river, they find barges, ferryboats and a trading boat for a 3,000-kilometer, month-long journey down the huge river to Iquitos and Manaus.

On through the Matto Grosso to Bazilia, Rio and Sao Paulo, Iguasu Falls, Montevideo and Buenos Aires, before hitching for much of the way south through Patagonia to the amazing glaciers of southern Argentina, the Magellan Straits and Tierra del Fuego. Here they reach the southernmost city in the world, Ushuaia, Six months, 17 countries, 23,000 kilometers: endless school projects for the kids.

ACROSS THE SOUTH PACIFIC
Iain Finlay & Trish Clark

Leaving Santiago, Chile after a frightening night of earth tremors, Iain, Trish and their two children, now 12 and 13 years old, fly to Easter Island, where, using their own tents, they camp out in remote corners of the island as they explore the huge, enigmatic stone monoliths. From there, its Tahiti and the stunning beauty of Bora Bora, Morea and the unbelievable Tuamotu atolls. In the Cook Islands they board a copra trading vessel for a journey through the island chain; Aitutaki, Rakahanga and Manihiki. When it breaks down, mid-ocean, they go overboard with the crew to swim in water 3,000 metres deep. American and Western Samoa are next, in the midst of a typhoon. Then the pleasures and beauty of Tonga, the Fiji Islands, Vanuatu and New Caledonia, before finally returning to their home in Australia. The message about travelling with your kids is: do it before their teens. By then its too late. Ian & Trish only just made it.

GOOD MORNING HANOI
Iain Finlay & Trish Clark

When Iain Finlay and Trish Clark arrive in Hanoi on a one-year work assignment for the English language service of the communist government-run radio network, they can hardly foresee the intense and exceptional experiences that await them. Coming to Vietnam for an Australian aid agency, their intended role is to coach and instruct, or at least to share their knowledge, with a small group of young reporters. But they find that they learn more than they teach.

As friendships with their colleagues grow, Iain and Trish are involved in developing and presenting a daily radio program - the first run by Westerners on a regular basis - and they become immersed in the stimulating life of one of Asia's most enchanting cities. In the process, they gain fascinating insights into Vietnamese society and culture, as well as a greater understanding and respect for the new Vietnam.

Good Morning Hanoi also illuminates the lives of a group of people dwelling in crowded conditions around a small courtyard in central Hanoi where Iain and Trish find a house to rent, and who become like an extended family living in the heart of the city.

In *Good Morning Hanoi*, Iain and Trish, two of the founders and producers of the international television program *Beyond 2000*, return to a country from which they had reported during the Vietnam War. They find an extraordinarily friendly people whose resilience and irrepressible good nature enable them to put the past behind them and move into the future with confidence.

(Illustrated. Available now: <highadventureproductions.com>)

THE SILK TRAIN
Iain Finlay & Trish Clark

The Silk Train is travel adventure with a geo-political backbone. Veteran journalists Iain Finlay and Trish Clark set out to travel 21,000 kilometres from Singapore to Venice, by hopping on and off trains up through South East Asia, across China, Central Asia, the Caucasus, Turkey and the Balkans. Much of their route covers territory along which the ancient Silk Road trails wound their way over the past two thousand years. They planned to use rail lines that form part of an embryonic, UN-backed Trans-Asian Railway network, that will eventually create unbroken freight and passenger corridors all the way from China's far-eastern seaboard, to Europe.

While visiting some of the great historic sites of China and Central Asia, among them: Xi'an, Dunhaung, Samarkand and Bukhara, they also become aware of the changing dynamics of Big-Power politics across the vast Central Asian steppes, once the stamping grounds of Genghis Khan and Tamerlane, which now include the newly independent countries of Kazakhstan, Kyrgyzstan and Uzbekistan. They very quickly realise that, by far the most important items of trade along the modern equivalents of the Silk Road, are now oil and natural gas. Oil is the new silk. It is the new trans-national currency of the Silk Road, with China and its voracious, seemingly insatiable appetite for energy, emerging as the most significant factor in the political and economic arena of Central and South East Asia.

Further west, Russia's increased pressure on the Caucasus, particularly Georgia, is just another indication of how vital the world's dwindling energy resources are and will remain for most of the twenty-first century. By journey's end, in Venice, they realise they have travelled a very different Silk Road than that of Marco Polo.

(Illustrated. Available now: <highadventureproductions.com>)

Imperiumbooks.com
Highadventurepublishing.com
and
Highadventureproductions.com

are part of
High Adventure Productions Pty. Ltd.
PO Box 111
Tumbulgum, NSW 2490
email: iaintrish@mac.com
AUSTRALIA